Wanted for Killing

A RINEHART SUSPENSE NOVEL

Wanted for Killing

by John Welcome

A RINEHART SUSPENSE NOVEL

Holt, Rinehart and Winston
New York   Chicago   San Francisco

Copy 1 ✓

First published in the United States in 1967

Library of Congress Catalog Card Number: 67-10080

First Edition

89290-0117
Printed in the United States of America

Wanted for Killing

A RINEHART SUSPENSE NOVEL

1

Destroy when Memorized

I was watching a shoal of fat, striped, friendly-looking fish. They were making their silent, effortless way between the chasms and gorges, the peaks and luxuriant valleys of the Corsican sea bed. Below them some form of crustacean moved. I put my head down to see better. The glass clouded over and water poured in from somewhere. I began to suffocate. Sea water shot up my nose and I had that moment of silly, irrational panic which comes to all inexperienced snorkelers. I ripped off the mask, kicked, and came up. There was a laugh from the beach.

"I'm the world's most useless underwater operator," I said. "If that is the right word." I swam a few strokes, put down my feet, and waded ashore.

Sue and Simon Herald were lying in the sun on beach mats. Facing me as I walked toward them, the sand hot beneath my feet, was the whole glorious expanse of the Bay of Ajaccio.

"This is what might loosely be described as the life," I said as I threw myself down beside them. "Do you plan to stay here permanently or is it only for the summer and the sun?"

Sue sat up and looked at her husband. "We don't quite know yet," she said slowly.

7

"I never guessed it was quite so lovely," I said. "And the peace and the lack of crowds. It's like the West Indies on your doorstep, only better."

"The trouble is too many other people are beginning to find that out," Simon said. "It's always the same, isn't it? Every time one gets hold of something one wants, the rest of the world seems to want it too."

"Yes, but Simon, there are not exactly *many* others about, are there?" Sue said.

The crescent of golden sand stretching for the best part of half a mile was deserted save for the three of us. There were, it is true, large boards bearing the inscription *Propriété privée —Défense d'entrer* at either end.

Simon saw me looking at them. "Yes," he said. "A year ago there was no necessity for them. Now, in additon, one has to put up a regular barbed-wire entanglement to keep people out, and even that often isn't much use. Well, I'm going up. I've got some letters to write."

Getting to his feet, he walked toward the gate at the head of the beach. Then he went on along the path between the palms and the mimosa, crossed the terrace, and entered the house. He had bought it a year back after wandering about for some time when his first marriage collapsed, modernized it, and tinkered with it and improved it because he liked playing with houses. Then he and Sue Marston, his second wife, had, for the present at any rate, made it their home.

Sue stared after him, a little frown, of which she was almost certainly unaware, appearing between her eyes. She turned to me. "Come on," she said, "let's swim again. I'll race you to the rocks."

There was a clump of them in the center of the little bay and she beat me to them quite comfortably, as I knew she would. When I reached her, she was settling herself on the largest which was shaped rather like a reclining chair, its surface smooth and polished by the sun and sea water. Drops of water glistened on her skin between the negligible strips of material she wore across her loins and breasts. She had long shapely legs and

8

thighs; her hair had a tint of auburn in it. She was a very pretty girl and she looked unhappy.

The mountains surrounded the bay. Far across it a pale line of white showed the harbor installations of Ajaccio. To the right, above Vizzavona, even now in July, there was snow on the peaks, for it had been a hard winter. Down here the sun was blazing out of a cloudless sky. The water through which we had come was warm on the skin.

I had been with the Heralds for over a week. After Geoffrey Wainwright had left me to go his own mysterious ways I had found a small pension in Ile Rousse overlooking the port and had stayed on there eating superb food, lying in bed late in the mornings, and in the sun and the sea in the afternoons, getting stronger every day. Then I had called Simon and more or less wished myself on them. I had come down to Ajaccio in the strange little train which runs through the very center of the island. Even I, who thought I had been everywhere and seen everything, had been almost blinded by the beauty which lay around every twist and curve of the track. They had met me in Ajaccio and driven me out to the villa, pressing me to stay as long as I liked. And it had not taken me more than a day to feel that something was wrong, although, in a way, I had known it already.

Simon Herald was a very old friend of mine. We had served for a bit in the same regiment and had afterward met each other in more independent employment. He had raced motor cars while I had ridden steeplechases, and we had pulled each other's legs about our respective passions. Then he had smashed himself up at Le Mans, contracted a disastrous first marriage, and gone to live in Ireland, so that I had lost touch with him for a while. After his divorce he had been often in London and we had spent much of our time together. He was a year or so older than I was and Sue was considerably younger, so that there was a biggish gap between their ages. When he married her, our mutual friends had given it about a year. In fact Sue's brother, Roddy, an up-and-coming rider, at a time when I was down and going, had made book on it.

Fond as I was of them both, I had had my own doubts. Simon, I knew, was no easy trick when it came to the business of living together; and Sue, besides being very young, had a will of her own. Now I was uncomfortably afraid that some of my doubts might be coming home to roost.

Sue stretched in the sun like some lithe young animal. "You don't know how privileged you are, Richard," she said. "I regard these rocks as my very own. Often in the mornings I lie here for hours roasting myself all over."

"I see. Well, don't let my presence deter you."

"Shut up, debauchee. I know all about you. Why did you never get married, Richard?"

"I tried to once not so long ago. She wouldn't have me. Said I was too independent a type. I didn't need her, she said."

"I expect she was a pretty independent type herself. Those sort of women always want weepies. It wouldn't have worked."

"You're probably right." I suddenly didn't want to discuss it any more. The scar was rawer than I had thought.

"You've been up to something, Richard, haven't you? Those are bullet wounds in your shoulder and leg, aren't they? Simon says they are, and he ought to know. Fairly recent ones, so he says."

"Well, he's right and so are you. But I'm supposed not to talk about it."

And I am not going to talk about what I am doing or supposed to be doing now either, I told myself. For my conscience wasn't entirely clear as to the terms on which I was the guest of my friends.

The pension where I had stayed at Ile Rousse had been a small building just outside the village, almost in the sea, over which geraniums and bougainvillea ran in cheerful riot. The patron was a huge friendly man who came originally from the Department of War and who had served with the Resistance in the Alpes Maritimes during the war. He fed me great luscious meals on the terrace from which I could also swim. Because I slept a lot during the day I sat up late into the night, and since

10

le patron stayed with me, behind the bar, refilling my glass, we had become friendly and talked together.

We had discussed le Président, his influence on Corsican affairs, and how he had settled the Algerian problem. This indeed affected le patron and everyone in Corsica more directly than anything else he had done. All along the east coast of the island, he told me, the colons had been resettled in considerable numbers and were now in the process of reforming into what was almost a new little colony of their own. In addition, of course, there was the Legion, with its depots in Bonifacio and Corte.

Le patron wasn't sure about the Legion. It was true they had brought in spending money to help out the tourist trade and to keep things going in the winter when that was slack. But they had brought their own problems with them too. There had been incidents when they had first arrived, men out on leave or weekend passes wrecking cafés and the like. Things had been tightened up since then; now only the good characters were allowed to go a distance from their depots; the roustabouts and the wild ones were kept within easy reach of their own military police. They were not pleasant people to tangle with, legionnaires when they had wine in their blood.

"I'm surprised le Président didn't disband them," I said.

Le patron thought that would have been an admission of failure which le Président, of course, could not endure. Or again he might have ideas of using them as a sort of *force de frappe* of his own if the time came.

"A sort of Praetorian Guard," I said. "I wonder. I'm afraid the world has no use for them any more. They're soldiers of fortune."

"Yes, but whose fortune, M'sieu? That's what we often talk of here. Le Président deceives himself if he thinks they are all his men. Some of them now serving have never forgiven him for Algeria and what they call the betrayal, and they never will. And, in their cups, the reckless ones—and what legionnaire is not reckless, M'sieu—say so."

11

Then, as if he thought that he had said too much, he had begun to ask me about myself. I gave him off-hand answers. He had seen my passport, and I was all too conscious that the vital embarkation and entry stamps were missing from it for the very good reason that my departure from England had been hurried, illegal, and almost fatal, and that I had come ashore here quietly from a yacht. He was bound to be curious, and someone, I supposed, was bound to catch up with me pretty soon.

Once or twice, too, I caught le patron studying me as I swam or rested in the sun. If he recognized the raw marks as bullet wounds he never mentioned them—at least to me. But of course he did speak to someone. I never knew just who it was or how it was managed. That it happened was enough. And, I suppose, given certain people and their wounded feelings, it was a certainty that it would. They had me over a barrel after all.

As I felt better and grew stronger I began to walk into the village for my pre-dinner drinks. There, at the Café de Platanes in the square, I would sit and sip and watch the life of the little town flowing past me.

One evening I was sitting underneath the plane trees, the soft, mild, caressing air of the place all about me, when someone stopped at my table. I knew what he was before he spoke or I looked at him. You get so that you can feel their presence, like a crook smelling a copper, especially when you've been in the business yourself.

"I will join you in a drink, Mr. Graham," he said in English which bore only the faintest trace of an accent. He pulled out a chair and sat down, beckoning a waiter as he did so.

I did look at him then. He was wearing a gray lightweight suit of a type which can be bought ready-made in any big store. His shirt and tie were nondescript. So were his features, just enough tinged with the sun to be unremarkable; no one would notice him in a crowd. He was one of the faceless ones all right. I sighed. They could never leave you alone once they

12

had you. Here we go again, I thought. I finished my pastis and, when the waiter came, told him to bring me another. I thought I might need it.

He waited for the waiter to move away. Then his glance left me and went on around the place, ascertaining our distance from other tables. It lingered on two legionnaires who were drinking Kronenburg over near the roadway. "Le-Képi-blanc," he said, running the words together as the French do. "Have you ever served with them, Mr. Graham?"

"No. I've done most things in my time, but not that."

"Ah, so much the better perhaps. They are the best soldiers in the world, but *un peu fous.*" He tapped his head. "It is *le cafard,* I think," he said.

"Yes," I said.

"Mr. Graham, we find ourselves in a little difficulty. We want your help."

"I'm here on holiday."

"Well, an enforced holiday perhaps. How are you feeling?"

"Pretty fit on the whole."

"Good. You see, Mr. Graham, I know all about your recent activities. In case you doubt my credentials I will tell you."

"I'll be interested in that."

"You left England in a very unorthodox way. You were mixed up in violence in which a man died. You were wounded. You are in a difficult and indeed dangerous position. We could take you now and hand you back to the English authorities. In fact, that is what we should do."

"The English authorities mightn't thank you for me," I said, "in view of all the things I can say."

"No, possibly. But, you know, I think we could embarrass you considerably here, Mr. Graham. Something to do with illegal entry and other interesting things. Have you ever been in a Corsican jail, Mr. Graham?"

"No. I can't say I'm anxious to try."

"We didn't think you would be."

"How do you know all this?"

"We work together with certain English—shall we say—institutions, as indeed you are aware, none better. I have had a letter setting out the facts."

"I can guess who wrote it," I said bitterly. "A blind carbon, I suppose?" Bloody old Bellamy up to his tricks again, I thought.

He did not smile; his expression had not and did not change throughout the interview. But he ordered another pastis. So did I.

"He requested us to keep an eye on you," he said. "He suggested—no more—that we might make use of you."

"And if I go along with you?"

"Then I think I can say that you will be able to return to the United Kingdom without another thought and live there as you wish. You would not care to be an exile forever?"

"What have you got for me to do?" I asked him.

"You are going to stay with friends in a few days."

For the first time I sat up. "How the devil do you know that?"

"But, Mr. Graham, surely you know the telephone exchanges in these islands are very primitive? The operators are badly paid. They are only too glad to be of assistance to us in respect to certain calls."

"I see. Go on."

"Your friend, Simon Herald, finds himself in an uncomfortable position. There are people who want his house. We know the people, or a few of them. They are mixed up in something very dangerous and very unsavory. We wonder. We wonder why they want his house. We watch these people as carefully as we can. They are clever. We only know a little and guess a little at what they are doing. It is not enough. We are short of trained men. I find myself handicapped. I must know—we must know—Mr. Graham, why they want that house. It is very simple. Perhaps you will find out for us."

"Is Simon mixed up in this?"

"I would say not. I understand he is proving difficult. He is reluctant to part with the property. But all that you will find out, please."

"I won't spy on my friends."

14

"You will be helping them. They are in a difficult situation."

"Hmm."

"Remember, for this service you will be allowed back. I assume that at present you are not too sure of your reception if you do return?"

He was right there. I wasn't.

As he got to his feet he laid a piece of pasteboard before me on the table.

JACQUES DEFORGE, I read. IMPORTS AND EXPORTS. There were addresses and telephone numbers in Ajaccio and Bastia.

"Destroy when memorized," he said. "Use the Ajaccio number. Before saying anything remark upon the weather. Make sure whoever answers does so as well."

He pushed back his chair. A few steps and he had mingled with the plutocracy from the Napoleon Bonaparte who were promenading up and down the side of the square. Then, like a shadow, he had gone. It was quite neatly done. But before he faded from view I had time to notice that he was wearing those black-and-white golfing shoes. I didn't know they were made any more. It was a streak of individuality I thought he should not have permitted himself. That and the drinking of three pastis during a short conversation made me wonder if he was a good agent. Probably not. The shoes bothered me. Besides, they were unlikely to employ a top man in this out-of-the-way place. That he was genuine I had no doubt at all.

So here I was, not all that happy in my own mind just as, I was now finding out, my friends were not happy in theirs, though for different reasons.

2

The Lake

Sue's voice broke into my thoughts. "Richard, did you know Simon's first wife?"

"Mildred? Yes, of course."

"What was she like?"

"She was a tiger bitch."

"I thought so. Richard, do you think she could be up to something now?"

I nearly fell off the rock. "Mildred? Not an earthly chance, I should say. The last I heard of her, she was living with that chap who runs her horses for her, and quite content to all appearances."

"Well, you must have seen Simon is all on edge. He's been getting letters he won't show me. I know that. He's been snappy and jumpy and goes off into long silences, and I can't get near him any more."

"I still don't think it's Mildred. Could it be money?"

"Good God, no. He's rotten with cash. You know that. Look, Richard, I'm only too well aware that everyone said I'd never handle Simon. I know there were bets on how long we'd last together. Everyone told me I was insane to marry him. Well, I'm in love with him, Richard. I think I've been in love with him

16

ever since I first met him that night in Avignon. When he left me in that hotel in Arles I wanted him to stay and sleep with me. I knew I wanted him and that I'd never let him go. And I was a virgin then, believe it or not. Can you understand this?"

"Yes, I think so."

"I'm still in love with him. And it *has* worked. It's been a case for the books and all our kind friends were wrong. And he's still in love with me. I know he is. But something is eating hell out of him, and he won't tell me what it is. Richard, will you help?"

"What do you want me to do?"

She sat up and put her hands around her knees. "Ask him what's gotten into him, what's gone wrong. He's more likely to tell a man, and you know him better than anyone."

"Yes, but Susan, the old boy isn't the easiest to approach on his private affairs. He's just as likely to tell me to go to hell in a handbasket."

"Richard, please. You're the only hope I have. He's getting worse. And another letter came today. I know it did. I saw him slide it out of the mailbox. I don't give a damn if he's being blackmailed. I don't care what he has done, if he'd only open up."

"I doubt very much if he's being blackmailed. All right, Sue. I always was a sucker for a pretty girl. I'll do my best."

"Before dinner tonight? Richard, please."

"All right. But put out plenty of whiskey."

We walked together to the house. It was a fascinating place with red tiled roofs, big picture windows, a patio, and a terrace facing the sea. An old Genoese watchtower had been incorporated into the structure at one side.

I changed my clothes slowly, not a bit fancying the task which had been set for me. Still, I had made a promise and I pretty well had to keep it. Moreover, I had an idea I knew part of the answer. Then I made my way downstairs and crossed the huge living room which looked out on the terrace and the bay. A short passage led to the ground-floor room of the tower. Simon had converted this for his own use as a study and we usually had our pre-dinner drinks there.

The musket slits had gone and big windows had been cut into the deep stone walls. There were a couple of gun cases with Simon's Purdeys and two sporting rifles, one a big Mannlicher he'd had with him on safari. There were knee-high bookcases, deep leather chairs, and a club fender. On the stone mantelpiece was the sole reminder of Simon's short career as a racing driver, Sue's wedding present to him, an exquisite silver-and-bronze model of a four-and-a-half blower Bentley, the car in which as an undergraduate he had started his career and which he always said was the most romantic and exciting motor car ever built.

He was there all right, sitting on the club fender reading or, I imagine, rereading, a letter. As I came in he folded it up and thrust it into a pocket.

I could hardly ask him what his correspondence was about. I was damned if I knew how I was going to lead up to the subject at all. As I had told Sue, and which she very well knew, he wasn't the easiest to approach on matters near to himself, and he was quite likely to remind me in strong terms that his personal business was his own affair, which it was.

But there was no doubt about his being edgy. At my entrance he got to his feet and started walking around the room, picking things up and putting them down. He stopped in front of one of the windows and stared out at the view, his hands deep in his trouser pockets, apparently quite abstracted. Then, suddenly remembering my presence, he turned back to the room.

"Hello, Richard," he said vaguely, "have a drink?"

"Yes, in a moment," I said. "I'll probably need one. Look, Simon, I know it's none of my damn business, but is there anything up? I . . ."

He didn't seem to hear me. There was no doubt at all about it—he was either vague or deaf or distracted. The last seemed the most probable. It was all very unlike him. I wondered what the hell had been in that letter.

"Come and take a stroll outside," he said. "You've never really seen the property, have you?" Without waiting for an answer he led the way along the passage to the main door which faced away from the sea toward the mountains.

Drawn up a little to one side of the doorway were Simon's and Sue's cars—a Porsche ("Just the thing for these roads, old boy.") and a Renault Caravelle. There was a Land Rover somewhere around, too. Simon believed in doing well in the way of cars.

To our left a short curving drive led up to a Moorish archway that gave onto the little-frequented road. Simon turned away from it and took a path between clumps of cacti.

He had been right when he said that I had never really seen the place, for I had spent most of my time either lazing in a long deck chair on the terrace or on the beach or in the sea. The place was much more extensive than I had thought.

It had belonged originally, Simon said, to one of the old Corsican families, whose vast, ornate, above-ground mausoleum was still there tucked away into a corner of the property. Then, just before the war, it had been bought by a right-wing French tycoon about whom very little seemed to be known, and from whose family or representatives Simon had purchased it.

There was a vineyard of sorts, which Simon played around in when he had nothing better to do and in which a couple of men were working, but most of the land was rough and covered with scrub, called maquis by the Corsicans, through which sandy paths had either been cut or had just come about. I suppose there must have been about ten acres all told and it occupied the entire area of a little headland. The house and the beach on which we had been lying were sheltered by a low ridge which, Simon told me, cut them off from the *libecchio,* the wind that sometimes came out of the southwest and blew for days and when it did was the curse of the island. On the far side of the ridge the ground was barren and sloped down to rocks and low cliffs and the sea.

We walked along here for a bit and then turned inland again. Suddenly we came out of the maquis onto a broad level space. In the center of this space was a large, almost circular pool or lake. The sides of this lake were sharp and clearly defined as if they had been cut by hand, and a tiny gravel beach about two feet wide surrounded it.

19

But it was the surface of the lake itself which commanded attention, for it was utterly unlike any of the waters around. Instead of the welcoming translucency of the sea, this was dark and opaque and quite impenetrable to the eye. It was also dead flat and calm, with the matte color of an old coin. All around and above it the air was quite still, and the lake and its immediate surroundings appeared to repel the bright, cheerful sunlight. I suddenly wanted to shiver. There was a sinister feeling about the whole place as if here were secrets it was better not to know. I remembered that the origins of Corsica went back to the womb of time.

More to turn away from the unpleasant stretch of water than anything else, I looked around me. To my left, a few hundred yards away was a small hill. Sitting on top of it on an outcrop of rock, in full view, was the figure of a man. He was using a pair of field glasses and they were trained directly upon us. It was a sufficiently odd situation to make me remark on it.

"We have company," I said to Simon.

He looked up so quickly that I almost thought he must have been expecting something. Seeing the man, he stiffened and half-stopped in his stride. Then he relaxed and took me quietly by the arm.

"Just walk on for the moment as if we hadn't seen him," he said.

He led me over to the edge of the lake and along the little shore. We came to where a rock jutted out, high enough to hide us. Simon bent down and started to pick up flat stones. Then, idly, he began the child's game of skimming them across the surface of the water.

"Lean against the rock just enough to show yourself," he said to me. "Chuck these stones in now and then and behave as if I was still here. I'm going to try to work around him." He pushed the stones into my hands. Then, bending double, he ran along the beach. After a bit, when he was beyond the hill and, I supposed, out of the watcher's range of vision, he climbed up and disappeared into the maquis.

I did as I was told, leaning against the rock with a portion of my body exposed to view. Every now and then I skimmed a stone across the dark surface of the lake. Closer acquaintance did not increase my liking for it. Even the stones seemed unwilling to skim, bouncing once or not at all and being swallowed up immediately.

After a little I thought I had been inactive long enough and that I might as well see for myself if anything was going on. Turning around, I looked back up the hill.

The watcher had disappeared, but Simon was running as hard as he could through the paths in the maquis, back toward the house. I hoisted myself onto the turf and followed him. As I ran I could hear the faint phut-phut of a scooter from the road.

When I reached a point where I could look down to the house, Simon was opening the driver's door of the Porsche. The engine came to life and I ran for the gateway.

As he came under the arch he caught sight of me and slowed down for a second. Jerking open the other door I slid in beside him.

"Flushed the fellow all right," he said, "but too bloody soon. He must have spotted me. He's only got a scooter. We're bound to catch him." He set the Porsche going along the narrow empty road.

Simon was right, of course. We *were* bound to catch him. He couldn't have had more than a couple of minutes start and the Porsche was doing seventy in third almost as soon as I had settled myself in the seat. The road ran by the sea past thick growths of maquis or along empty golden beaches. But the thing was, we didn't.

One or two cars met us going the other way. The only thing we caught and passed was a truck bumping along. We went all the way to the bridge at Pisciatello, but there was no scooter on the road.

"Well, I'm damned," Simon said, pulling up the car at the bridge. "He can't have come as far as this."

"There are one or two gaps in the maquis," I said. "He could have pulled in there perhaps."

21

"It's just possible, though I doubt if he'd have had time. If he has, we've lost him."

The truck chugged past us and took the road to Propriano. It was painted a claret color and, almost unconsciously, I took in the fact that it seemed smarter than most Corsican vehicles.

"There's a tavern we passed," I said. "Could he have run in there?"

"He might. I doubt it. The old girl who runs it is rather a chum of ours. Still, we can try." He turned the car and we proceeded rather more slowly back the way we had come.

The Bar Des Amis consisted of a tiny house with a cement platform in front of it surrounded by wire netting after the manner of a prisoner-of-war cage. Above the wire netting was a blue-and-white banner bearing the name in large letters. The formica-topped tables which dotted the platform were empty except for one person, an old lady dressed in black. She was seated in a wicker chair, her hands in her lap, staring out to sea.

"Doesn't look very promising. Just the same we might have a beer," Simon said. He turned the car into a yard beside the building and we both got out. Instead of going immediately around to the bar Simon crossed the yard. The place only consisted of a few sheds and it was the work of a moment to run our eyes over them. There were chickens and a goat and dogs, one of whom was tied up and barked, but no scooter.

The old girl came over to us as soon as we sat down and greeted Simon. He ordered two beers and, when they came, the glasses cool and misted from the ice, he asked her to sit down with us. They talked local gossip for a while: how the cook had walked out of the holiday village and the young wife of a nearby hotelier in the hills was cheating with the manager. Then Simon asked her about the scooter.

No, she said. She had seen a scooter going down our way an hour or so ago, but not coming back. She gave Simon a questioning look. "You have been having some trouble with trespassers, M'sieu?" she said.

"Well, yes," Simon admitted, reluctantly, I thought.

She looked at him again. "It is not a happy house," she said.

22

"Some are like that. They carry trouble with them for all who live in them. It has a sad history. Whatever changes you make you cannot take that away." She did not turn her head as she spoke, but sat quite still, almost like a figure out of the stone age herself with her carved aquiline features, her hands folded in her lap, her eyes staring out over the ancient sea.

"Hmm," Simon said, putting down his glass. "Come on, Richard, we'd better be going." He got to his feet and went out to the car.

"And now," I said to him as we turned under the archway spanning the drive, "perhaps you'll tell me what this is all about."

"Perhaps. I wonder where Sue is." He stopped in the middle of the great room which faced the sea and shouted, "Sue!"

From somewhere upstairs came the call, "Yes, do you want me?"

"No, it's all right." He let out a little sigh of relief. "They weren't drawing me off then," he said. "I suddenly thought I might have walked right into it."

Feeling more than a bit mystified, I followed him into the study. He poured a whiskey and handed it to me.

"Well," I said, "you can tell me to go to hell if you like, but Sue is as worried as all get out on account of you. What *is* going on?"

He stared at his glass. "That's just the trouble," he said, "I only wish I knew."

3

Fish in Deep Waters

"Well now I'll be damned," I said. "You take off after some bird-watcher like a hound out of hell and then you say you don't know what's going on."

"He wasn't a bird-watcher. I wish it were as simple as that. So Sue is worried, is she?"

"More than a little, Simon."

He kept on staring moodily at his glass and swirling the ice cubes around in it. "I should have told her, I suppose," he said. "The thing was I didn't know whether to bother her about it or not. It was so bloody nebulous. And then it got worse. We've been so happy here, you know. That's all nonsense what the old girl said about it being an unhappy house. Perhaps she's in it too. You see, Richard, well, after Mildred, I could never believe I could be happy with a woman again. And then Sue being so much younger than I am, I thought it unfair to burden her with my moods. I knew everyone said I wasn't made for marriage and that it wouldn't work, and you know I half-believed them to be right. But, by God, it has worked. I found this place by accident and Sue loved it from the start. I've never had such peace and happiness in my life, and it all seems bound up with the place and just being ourselves here and living quietly and, oh, dammit, I don't know if you can understand . . ."

24

"I can have a shot at it."

"Now someone is trying to take the place away from me."

"What?"

"It's a fact. It all started about a month ago when a little man from the agency in Ajaccio came out and asked me if I'd sell. I thought it was just a routine inquiry and I refused. He said he was prepared to offer me a good profit. Out of interest I asked him what it was. It fairly staggered me. It was about five times what I'd paid for and spent on the house. I turned him down. He asked me not to sell to anyone without letting him know, as his client was very interested, and breezed off."

"Well, that's ordinary enough, I suppose. Aren't prices soaring here?"

"Yes, but not quite as much as that. The next thing that happened was that I got a letter from a solicitor in Ireland, of all places. As a matter of fact I knew the chap. He's one of the fashionable Dublin solicitors and acted for us over there. He, too, wanted to know if I'd sell. I didn't bother to answer the letter and a week later there was a follow up. I wrote and said it wasn't on the market and wasn't likely to be. Then things began to happen."

"What sort of things?"

"Silly things at first. Weekenders straying by mistake on to our private beach; my tires having the air let out of them in Ajaccio; a couple of anonymous letters. Then rather more trying things. A Foreign Legion tough trying to pick a fight with me at the Casino, a waiter tipping some scalding soup over me at dinner, trucks bringing our supplies being delayed or just not turning up. Finally, last Sunday, the beach below was invaded by a gang of practically naked thugs with transistors and girl friends and all the fittings. I went down and told them to get out. They were most of them tight and they laughed at me. I'd had just about enough of things by this time. I came back here and got a gun." He nodded toward the gun racks. "Sue, mercifully, was out. I shoved in a couple of number eight shot and went down to the beach again. They thought I was bluffing and the biggest of them decided to call me. He was wearing what is called in best

25

naturist circles a minimum and nothing else. He was about the size of Nelson's Column and covered with hair. I waited until he was a yard or so away and then I put the choke barrel into the sand at his feet. You can imagine what happened. He'll be picking sand out of himself for the rest of his life I should think. It must have hurt like hell. He screamed and doubled over. The rest of them must have thought I'd killed him. They didn't waste much time getting out. They even forgot to take their transistors."

"Christ, Simon, you took a hell of a risk."

"I was in a mood for taking risks." He looked just then as he must have looked at certain times during the war and when he'd had the gun in his hands on the beach. I wasn't surprised they hadn't stopped to face further powder and shot.

At that moment Sue came in. "Dinner is ready if you are," she said.

None of us spoke much over the meal which was served in the big room, the lights of Ajaccio making a sort of spangled backdrop across the bay. When we had finished, Sue left us for a few minutes.

"You'll have to tell her," I said. "Maybe if the three of us kick it around we can make some sort of sense out of it."

"Yes. I didn't realize I was showing it so obviously."

"I don't think one ever does. In any event when someone is in love with you, they can spot things pretty quick. You don't realize how bloody lucky you are."

"I do. That's just the trouble. Shove along that brandy, will you?"

"Could all this have anything to do with the lake we saw that chap watching? Isn't there some legend of Rommel's treasure having gone astray somewhere in Corsica?"

"There is, but not here. It was up near Bastia at the other end of the island. I don't believe there ever was any Rommel's treasure, but even if there was, it came nowhere near here and was sunk in the sands off the Golo River long ago. You're right about Sue; let's go along."

Back in the round room, deep in our armchairs with a bottle

of Martell between us, he did tell her, right down to the incident of the afternoon and the disappearing scooter.

She drew a deep breath. "Well," she said, "you can't believe what a relief it is to know. But why on earth is this being done?"

"There's something here which someone wants very badly," I said. "That's obvious. But what is it? I suggested to Simon it might be Rommel's treasure dumped into that lake."

She shivered a little. "It's the only thing about the place I don't like," she said. "It gives me the creeps. We tried to fill it in. Don't you remember, Simon, we had a skin-diver go down?"

"Yes," Simon answered, "and I've been thinking about that a bit since Richard mentioned the lake. All that business about the skin-diver was rather odd."

"I must say I didn't take to that ghastly little creep who got him for us."

Simon turned to me. "We both took an immediate dislike to the thing, just as you seem to have done," he said. "First of all I hired a firm of engineers to see if we could drain it and fill it in. Well, they weren't wonderfully efficient, but they did get it more or less drained—enough to show there weren't any boxes of bullion in it anyway—it's not all that deep, as it happens. But they said it would be a practical impossibility to fill it. It's fed by streams and springs and by the sea in some way. Their advice was that we'd only turn the place into a quagmire and cause ourselves God knows what trouble, so we gave up the idea."

"But we still hated it," Sue said.

"Yes, I can't altogether see why, but there it is. Anyway we were sitting in Ajaccio one evening over a drink talking about it, when a little man came up to our table."

"A perfectly horrid little man," Sue put in.

"Yes, well, I'm coming to that. I wish you'd let me tell this story."

"Sorry," Sue said with a grin and gave me a mischievous look.

They were nearer together than they had been for some weeks. The edge in the air had gone from between them, and they could bicker amicably once again.

"Where was I? Oh, yes, this little man came over. He apologized and said he had not been able to help overhearing what we had been saying and he thought perhaps he might be able to help. He also said he knew the place, as he'd been a friend of the people who had it before us. Neither of us liked him very much, I must say, but we didn't want to be downright rude and kick him out, so we listened. He said that he'd had dealings with the firm of engineers we'd employed and that they were incompetent—which we'd guessed already—and he suggested getting a skin-diver down. The diver could really explore the place and give us a proper report. He told us he had just the chap. It didn't seem a bad idea and I rather took to it."

"I didn't take to him," Sue said. "He kept fondling Simon's knee all the time he was talking."

"He's as queer as Dick's hatband all right," Simon went on. "And has a hide like a rhinoceros. He insisted on staying in our company and finally persuaded us to have dinner with him in the Plat d'Or."

"Who or what is he?" I asked.

"He's an Englishman called Shanks. He came to live here some years ago and built a place for himself beyond Propriano. This all came out during dinner, or as much of it as he wanted to, for he's no fool. He operates some sort of fishing concession out of Propriano. In the course of this or because of it—he skirted rather around this point—he comes in contact with the skin-divers on the island who are in any way connected with fishing."

"Skin-divers are mostly young, bronzed, and athletic, in case you don't know," Sue said.

"I don't know. I haven't any on my mailing list. Go on."

"He asked us over to his place the following day to meet the chap. Said he'd have us met in Propriano as it was rather hard to find his place. We'd all had rather a lot of drink by this time— he's the sort of food and drink snob you might imagine, calling for the chef and sending back the dishes and going through the motions with the wine list—but he succeeded in getting us a bit tight and we agreed to go."

"What happened?"

"A man of his picked us up in Propriano and it was just as well. The place is off the map, what maps there are of Corsica, that is. You go along an indescribable road until you go up along a sizeable sort of creek. There are yachts and launches and cruisers and God knows what moored in the creek, and they're all his as far as I could make out. One of them ferried us across. He certainly has built himself some place. It's a Moorish style mansion right on the sea."

"Roughly about the size of the Taj Mahal," Sue said.

"Coming along nicely that way, in any case. He had Buck's fizz and champagne cocktails waiting for us and damn good they were, too. He also had the skin-diver, a real beauty. He was an Italian looking boy called Guiseppe. A lot of the southern Corsicans have a strong Italian strain in them, and he was one of them. By the time Shanks had cured our hangovers and filled us up again, he'd gotten me to agree to let him come and operate the next day."

"You know, Simon, you're an ass," Sue said amicably.

"You weren't so far behind—maybe it was Guiseppe," Simon answered her. "Anyway they turned up all right and down Guiseppe went into the deep dark hole. In the end his report was just the same as the engineers'—there was nothing there and filling the lake would be a waste of time."

"Wait a moment," I said, something suddenly occurring to me. "Were you both there all the time the diver was down?"

Simon frowned. "Now you mention it," he said, "we weren't. Sue was looking after lunch and I was called away to the telephone."

"What sort of a call was it?"

"A long one about nothing from the mainland. It was a firm of wine shippers in Nice who had been given my name or said they had. I see what you're getting at . . ."

"Exactly. If they'd wanted him to, Guiseppe could have surfaced and given your Mr. Shanks quite a different report. Was it after this that the efforts to get hold of the place were stepped up?"

"I rather think it was. Another letter came today. It's from that solicitor chap I mentioned. Here it is . . ." He crossed to his desk and, taking up an envelope, handed it to me.

Inside was a letter written on thick, expensive, business writing paper with an embossed letterhead. It was a friendly, first-person letter stating that the writer had again had a very strong inquiry from clients of his who were interested in Simon's place, and wanting to know if he would reconsider his decision not to sell. It stressed that price was a minor consideration. The names of the clients were not disclosed. It also referred to previous letters.

"What did you do with the other letters?" I asked, "and what about these solicitors? It's a firm, I see."

"I put them in the wastepaper basket to answer the first part of your question," Simon said. "I don't know much about the firm. Someone told me about them when we went over. It's run by that chap Manahan who signed the letters. He bought and sold Newlands for us and did a few other things."

"It seems that whoever he's acting for is anxious to do business all right. Could it be Shanks?"

"It could, I suppose, but I don't see why he should go to Ireland to get a solicitor."

"Nor do I at the moment. But do you know, I rather think I'd like to meet your Mr. Shanks."

"That shouldn't be difficult. We gather he's in Propriano almost every evening having a drink and keeping an eye on his fishing interests."

"Fishing of all sorts and descriptions by the sound of him," I said.

4

Dick's Hatband

Next afternoon the three of us squashed into the Porsche and
set out for Propriano. We passed the bridge at Pisciatello,
where we had given up the chase yesterday, and took the road
ahead that climbed into the mountains. Up and up we went,
around narrow hairpin bends, with Simon swinging the car on
her front-wheel drive, going always that little bit faster than
the average driver and preserving at the same time that slight
extra degree of safety which comes from skill and from experience of real speed.

The incomparable maquis-covered, sweet-scented hills of
inner Corsica opened up before us. Always in the background
were the great snow-tipped peaks.

"The last, and the best, place in Europe," Simon said quietly
as we came under the chestnuts of the Col de St. Georges. Then,
in a few minutes, we were dropping down through the streets of
Olmeto, a deep blue sun-splashed inlet far below us. Simon turned left where we joined the highway along a curving
cliff road. We passed two modern hotels and then, all of a sudden, we were in the solitary street of the white-and-yellow fishing village of Propriano.

The parking lot was on the quayside. There were cafés with

big red-and-white parasols a few yards away; fishing boats were moored one against the other alongside the quay. The sea was a deep blue, and the hills rose all around it. We had met, I think, three cars on our fifty-mile journey, and there were very few people around. It was an enchanting little place.

"We'll have a drink here," Simon said, nodding to the umbrellas a few feet away, "and keep an eye out for him. If he comes, he does it in style. We won't miss him."

I stood for a moment beside the car, enjoying the warmth and the clear freshness of the air. And as I glanced around, something caught my eye and held it.

About fifty yards further down the street a truck was parked. It was a very smart truck and I can only say that it looked somehow familiar.

"You go on," I said to the others. "Is that a paper shop across the street? I've just remembered it was the King George VI at Ascot yesterday. Will I get an English paper there?"

"Yes, I imagine so. They're usually in by the afternoon."

I walked down the quayside. The truck was drawn up almost opposite the paper shop. The truck was the usual one of its type, angular and ungainly, differing only from most of its fellows, and indeed from the majority of Corsican vehicles, in that it was very smartly painted. I remembered my subconscious mental note about the smartness of the truck which had passed us yesterday. The color was the same too—claret with white number plates. And although again I had not registered the numbers, it seemed to me, though I couldn't be certain, that they were similar. A truck, of course, would have been a most adequate instrument for hiding a scooter and transporting its driver.

As I watched, I heard voices below me in one of the fishing boats. Someone was giving instructions, very definite instructions, about the disposal of the catch. Then a tousle-headed boy in jeans and a jersey appeared over the edge of the quay at a jump, crossed to the truck, got in and started the engine. The truck pulled away, swung around on its own length, chugged off up the street, turned to the right, and disappeared.

Very thoughtfully I went into the paper shop and bought the *Daily Telegraph*. A French horse called Chamonix had won, much as had been expected.

"Well?" Simon asked me, as I rejoined him.

"The French won it again," I said. "It's becoming a habit." I resolved to keep my suspicions to myself for the moment. In any case I had no time to impart them, for Simon looked up as I spoke.

"Hullo," he said, "he's arrived. Here's his nibs himself."

A huge, cream-colored Mercedes had drawn up beside the clump of umbrellas. A lithe and rather beautiful young man wearing a lightweight chauffeur's uniform sprang from the driving seat and whisked open the nearside rear door.

A small figure got out slowly and stood by the car. Even at a distance one could sense the air of self-importance which hung about him. He caught sight of us in an instant, indeed by the way he turned his glance in our direction I had the feeling he knew before he arrived that we were there. Making his way between the tables he came toward us. He was dressed à la mode in one of those Dior jerseys, exquisitely cut slacks, and rope-soled shoes, which had not been bought on the beach. The clothes were too much for him and made him look faintly ridiculous. That was my first impression of him. I was pretty sure he was corseted somewhere, but his thick silver mane of hair had remained undyed. He had a sharp little nose, very alert eyes of some indeterminate color, a high complexion, and a faint second chin which someone was clearly made to work upon to try to disguise the marks of years and good living. His manner was as near to mincing as one felt he dared to allow—at least in heterosexual company. His true age I put in the late fifties, and I was pretty sure I had seen him somewhere before.

"Ah," he greeted us, "my friends from Porticcio. How opportune."

"We have a visitor with us, Richard Graham. We're showing him something of Corsica," Simon said as he introduced me.

His little eyes flicked over me, summing me up, and sizing me up too, I thought. "Indeed," he said. "Well, Mr. Graham, you

33

have come to the right place. In all this lovely island I think the coast and the hinterland from here to Ajaccio surpass everything."

I made some noncommital reply, conscious that his eyes were on me. I racked my brains without success for the place of our previous meeting.

"We rather wanted to see you, as a matter of fact," Simon said, plunging straight into the object of the exercise, which I couldn't help thinking was a mistake. I glanced at Sue, and from the look on her face I gathered she thought so, too. When I turned back to Mr. Shanks, I wished I hadn't taken time to look at Sue. He missed nothing and there was little doubt that he had intercepted the glance. A sort of indefinable wariness had come over his features. Simon, I reflected, had always been a bit inclined to rush into things.

"That is complimentary indeed, but why, pray? Was there any special reason?"

"Do you remember that infernal lake or pond, or whatever you like to call it, we have near our house? You very kindly helped us to get a skin-diver to investigate it."

He gave an affected little shudder. "Yes, indeed I do. A horrible place, I thought. And why should we discuss it here? Let us all go along to the Roc E Mar and have something interesting to drink."

As he spoke, he was leaving his own chair and bending solicitously over Sue's. As she rose, he drew it back with a little flourish. Then he led the way to his car.

It was one of the new, immense Gross 600 Mercedes. As we got in I saw a thin claret band drawn along the body against the cream. Something clicked in my mind and I paused for a moment, staring at the juxtaposition of the colors. Then I entered the car. But I knew he had noticed that faint instinctive pause and followed the direction of my glance. He was altogether too alert, damn him.

Simon was talking to him interestedly about the car as it whisked us silently up the hill. I let my own thoughts roll back-

34

ward in time and studied Shanks as well as I could while they chatted. The trouble was that his eyes were never still, though in some strange way he managed to disguise their movement from the casual glance. Even while telling Simon about the car and patting his knee to emphasize his points, he was managing to include Sue and me in the conversation, to discuss the beauties of Propriano, to tell us of his own home, and to go on sizing me up.

"You must bring your friend to visit me, my dear Simon," he said. "We'll arrange a day soon, very soon. Monte Moncatini is arriving tomorrow for a night or so and goodness knows who or what he will bring along. But Monte is so amusing you could forgive him anything, the dear creature. And the divine Contessa has been with us for some time now. The Contessa di Maggiore, you know. Such a charming girl. You haven't met her? But you must. Ah, here we are."

We filed behind him through the narrow bar and on to the long terrace. It was on the very edge of the cliff and the whole bay lay directly below us. The hills rolled around us in color and splendor. A manager or under manager of some sort hurried up and hovered about.

"Champagne," Shanks said abruptly with a little wave of his hand. It came on the instant and the foaming liquid was poured into our glasses. Personally I would have preferred beer, but the wine was cold and dry.

"Ah, now to the skin-diver. And what do you want with him?"

"We thought we might have another go at the lake," Simon said. "And he's been down before. We decided he'd be the best chap to have."

"No doubt. But I know so many of them and they come and go. My little business brings me into contact with them. I am a fisherman, Mr. Graham," he went on, turning directly to me. "It's an occupation I find fascinating. Are you staying long?" His hand was on my knee now. I moved the chair back out of his range.

"Only a few days, I think," I said.

"And is it you who have encouraged Simon to get at the lake again?"

"Good heavens no. I only saw it for the first time yesterday. I didn't like it much. Perhaps some brigand chopped an enemy up and chucked him into it."

"Perhaps. Strange things happened here long ago. Some say they still do, you know."

"But this skin-diver chap," Simon ploughed on, "surely you remember him. Wasn't his name Guiseppe something or other?"

Shanks sipped his wine again. "Now you mention it, I believe it was Guiseppe," he said quietly. "Yes, Guiseppe. A wanderer, Simon. He was only here for a short time and did one or two jobs for me. He has gone drifting off somewhere else as these flotsam do—Sardinia, Elba, Italy, who knows."

"Well, that's that then," Simon said.

"Perhaps we could try again with another."

Simon was in a hole now. He'd pretty well asked for that one. Give him his due; he saw the trap and avoided it. "If we do decide to go ahead we certainly shall," he said.

"It makes it all the more imperative that you should come over for a drink with me to discuss the whole thing. It is indeed a pity I can't ask you today or even tomorrow, but with Monte arriving and you know what these Corsican servants are . . ." He gave a little shrug. "I have to see to everything myself. You are returning to your lovely home now?"

"Yes," Simon said.

"I shall telelphone you later in the evening, then. And now, forgive me for a moment while I ring my house to explain why I am late. They will always worry so about me, the dear loyal things. And these roads are so dangerous. You, my dear fellow," he laid his hand on Simon's shoulder, "you drive too fast. A legacy of your past, no doubt. Excitement and danger—they are so hard sometimes to do without, don't you think, Mr. Graham?" He hurried off to where the telephones were.

As soon as he was out of earshot Sue turned on Simon. "You

36

are an old ass," she said. "Why couldn't you have been a bit more subtle? Now he'll know we want to question Guiseppe and he'll take good care we don't."

"Only if there really is something Guiseppe told him that he's anxious to hide from us," Simon answered. "I think it's far better to push him into the open. What's your idea, Richard?"

"I thought at first it was a mistake. Now I'm not so sure you aren't right. I'll tell you one thing though. His name isn't Shanks."

"Oh, then what . . ."

But he was standing at the table. Rope-soled shoes, after all, make very little noise on tiled floors, especially if they are carefully used. He poured the rest of the wine. Raising his glass, he gave a little bow. "To our next meeting," he said, "and may it be soon. Especially with your dear lady, Simon. I long to take her away from you."

"You do say the nicest things, Mr. Shanks," Sue said. "Simon never says anything like that to me."

"Ah, but that's the trouble with marriage, isn't it? There's a place for you now in my car, should you so wish."

We all gave rather forced laughs and trooped outside into the sunshine.

5

Son et Guitares

"Well then, what is his name?" Simon asked as he started the car and sent her flying up toward Olmeto. "I want to kick the little brute every time I see him, I know that."

"He sends shivers down my spine," Sue said. "And I'm not sure if they are anti-sexual shivers, if you know what I mean, or sinister ones."

"His right name, or at least the name he used to go by, is Hamley-Richardson," I said. "He came into racing just before the outbreak of the war and had a fantastic run of luck. I remember well his being pointed out to me during the war, just when I started riding. Then the luck broke. He was betting, apparently, like a drunken sailor, as some of these chaps do when success hits them. He couldn't pay up. He was called at Tatts and blacklisted. I remember now hearing from somebody that he'd pulled up stakes, changed his name, and gone to Ireland. Quite a lot of those sort of chaps did, you know. There were good pickings to be had in Ireland in the war and just after it. You may have heard something about it when you lived there."

"Yes, I believe so, now you mention it. I never paid much attention to it. I had my own troubles, as you may recall. It's an

38

explanation perhaps of why the inquiry about the house should come from Ireland. How did you get on to him?"

"I was pretty certain I knew him. I couldn't for the life of me place him. The war is a pretty long time ago now. Then something fixed it for me."

"What?"

"It's amazing the vanity of some of these chaps. His racing colors were claret and white. His car is white, picked out in claret. And I'll tell you something else, that truck that was parked down the quay at Propriano was painted claret with white number plates. I'm all but certain it was the same one that was on the road when we were chasing the scooter. I suppose he's picked those distinctive colors for his enterprises here to remind him of his triumphs in the past."

"They could have shoved the scooter into the truck and made off."

"Exactly."

"Do you think he recognized you?"

"Your guess is as good as mine. But I doubt it. As I say, the war is a long way away and I was very small fry then. He's not the type to bother with beginners."

"No, but he's nobody's fool either. It does look as if he's in this thing, whatever it is, up to the neck. But I still don't see why he wants my house."

"Or the lake."

"You can take it from me it's not Rommel's treasure."

"I don't suppose it is, but I have a feeling there is something in it or about it."

"Let's try and get hold of Guiseppe ourselves," Sue said from the back. "Simon, do you remember that pub in Ajaccio where some of the skin-divers go? An English sailor we met told us about it after Shanks and Guiseppe had been at the lake. I do wish you wouldn't drive quite so fast on these roads."

"Sorry. I'm not concentrating either. Why the hell won't this chap get out of the way?"

We were over the pass and descending. Ajaccio lay far below, a cluster of white toy buildings in the sun. A Caravelle took off from the airport and climbed steeply over the bay. We were high above them all. In front of us a truck, laden with sacks, lurched and banged around the hairpins.

Simon put the flat of his hand on the horn and held it there. The truck swayed and held on, refusing to give way. Simon swore, knocked the Porsche into a lower gear, and began to edge into a position to pass. Suddenly, on a tiny piece of straight away, the truck driver seemed to hear him and give him room. Simon went for the gap.

At that moment a sack came off the truck and fell slap in front of us. I don't know how Simon missed it. As he swung the wheel another came down with a crash and burst open. The truck had come in again, closing the gap between it and the mountain wall.

Another sack came down. They weren't coming by accident. Someone was doing this, driving us toward the edge. I didn't know how fast we were moving, but I did know that only seconds and Simon's skill saved us from going over. And I recalled from the journey up there was a drop of a good two hundred feet hereabouts. Just to make sure, I suppose, another sack came down. I caught a glimpse of a tousled head in the gap it had left. It was only a glimpse, but I saw enough to recognize the boy who only an hour or so before had climbed into the truck.

It was Simon and the front-wheel drive between them that saved us. Somehow he held her, pivoted her on the brakes and the front wheels, and slid. We hit the last of the sacks, broadside on, with a crash. The Porsche tilted, lifted, and then settled back on the road. The truck went lurching on, rather faster than was strictly necessary, and then disappeared from view.

Simon stopped the car and we all sat quite still for the space of seconds.

Then, "All right, Sue?" Simon said very quietly.

"Yes, darling. Somewhere the shade of Nuvolari is taking off his hat."

40

He turned to me. "I suppose that truck is in his racing colors too," he said sourly.

"I was far too frightened to look."

"I rather think Mr. Shanks, or whatever his name is, owes us that drink."

We got out and examined the damage. The off-side front wheel, which had taken most of the trouble, was buckled, and the fender was bent. Otherwise we had gotten off lightly. The bags, we noticed with interest, bore no name and were filled with cement. We pushed them to one side and changed the wheel.

Simon drove, very slowly and carefully, back to Porticcio.

"He fixed it, of course, when he went off to telephone," I said a little later over drinks. "Whether he recognized me or not, he must have guessed I had seen through him."

"And that frightened him for some reason."

"That and our talk about the lake."

"I still don't get it. Dammit, I saw the lake emptied or all but emptied. There's nothing in it bigger than a ruddy rock."

"Simon, that ship's steward or ex-steward—he might know something," Sue said.

"It's an idea. He might. He's usually around the docks during the day and at Montaro's place in the evenings. I rather think he runs his business, whatever that may be, from there." He laughed and turned to me. "He's an engaging sort of ruffian," he said. "He was second steward on one of those yachts on charter that put in here. I forget her name. A London tycoon owns her and charters her to his chums at about two thousand a week when he doesn't want her. This steward chap, McKee, was swiping duty-free gin from the yacht to some of the cafés in the port. It's a well-known racket, as you probably know. But he got a bit overconfident. He was walking down the gangway with a suitcase full of the stuff in broad daylight when the owner himself stopped him. He was fired forthwith and was on the beach.

41

But he didn't go home, and how he fixed that one nobody knows. He's said to have gotten himself cut into every sort of deal from smuggling to resettling Algerians. If anyone knows where Guiseppe is or anything about him, McKee does."

"If Shanks is in the hurry he seems to be, the sooner we get hold of Guiseppe the better," I said.

"Why not tonight?" Sue said. "We could dine at the Plat d' Or."

"And tell the servants here that if Shanks rings up to say we haven't come back. That'll be just what he wants."

We had an excellent meal under the trees in the courtyard of the Plat d'Or. The *son et guitares,* of which Montaro's place was one, didn't, Simon said, get going until latish, and McKee wasn't likely to be alone until well into the night. So we lingered over our coffee and brandy, talking about old times together, but our conversation always came back to Shanks and the problem of what he wanted. Turn it over as much as we could and kick it around between us, we could not produce an answer. Finally we left and strolled up the Cours Grandval. The café was situated almost under the huge floodlit Napoleon Memorial.

We took our seats and ordered more drinks. The *son et guitares* were just warming up. "That's his table," Simon said, nodding to one corner. I noticed that a bottle of Black and White, a bowl of ice, and a carafe of water had been left on it in readiness for him. He was evidently an important regular customer.

After about half an hour he showed up. He was a big, blue-chinned man with a heavy, square face. He went quietly to his seat at the table. When he sat down he gave the occupants of the café a casual glance, then he dropped two lumps of ice into his glass and tipped about four fingers of whiskey over them. Swirling the whiskey around the ice for a moment he raised the glass to his lips and drank it off. After that he slowly poured another drink, this time adding water and leaving the glass untouched in front of him. All this was evidently something of a ritual. Simon waited until the second drink was ready, then he got to his feet and led us over to his table.

42

"Evening, Mr. Herald and madam. Evening, sir," he said, as I was introduced. "What are you all drinking tonight?"

He ordered us brandy, which came like lightning and in a bottle. We chatted about generalities for a bit and then Simon said, "Look, McKee, you know everyone in Ajaccio, don't you?"

The other man grinned, revealing a set of very white, even teeth. "Just about," he said. "That's part of my business."

"Well, I'm looking for a skin-diver called Guiseppe. He was down in a lake on my place a few weeks ago and I want to have a word with him."

McKee's face had suddenly grown serious. "That would be Guiseppe Portini," he said. "Used to hang out with Shanks over at Propriano mostly. I haven't heard where he's been lately. I dunno, Mr. Herald. I'll do what I can. Did you ask Shanks about him?"

"Yes. He says he's gone away. I'm not sure I believe him."

McKee grinned suddenly. "You might be right at that," he said. "Do you want a job done?"

"I might. In my lake. I want to know if it's really drainable or not."

He gave Simon a quick look. "Your lake, eh? That's there for keeps, Mr. Herald. I heard one of the men you had working on that drainage job talking about it once."

"Well, there it is. Do what you can, will you, McKee?"

"I'll see what I'm able to find out. I doubt if it'll be much."

We went home soon after that.

I spent most of the next day in the sea, thinking about nothing at all. When I came in from the beach after tea, McKee was in the living room talking to Simon. They both had serious expressions on their faces.

"Ah, there you are, Richard," Simon said. "Come on into the study."

We followed him along the flagged passage. Inside the room he produced whiskey and poured drinks. Then he turned to me. "Guiseppe is dead," he said abruptly.

"I see," I said. "That makes matters nice and complicated, doesn't it? What happened to him?"

Simon turned to McKee. "You're sure this is true?" he asked. For answer the big man took a wallet from his pocket. "Either of you gentlemen read Italian?" He slid a newspaper clipping out of the wallet and held it toward us.

"I do, a little," I said. I took the clipping. It was brief and I had no difficulty in understanding it. The few lines stated that a skin-diver, Guiseppe Portini, had been accidentally drowned due to failure of his apparatus when diving off Cagliari in Sardinia.

"There's not much doubt about that," I said, handing it back.

"What's more Mr. Herald," McKee went on, "I'm afraid your lake is poison. No one will operate in it. I tried around for you, but something's up. They just won't come near the place."

"Well, I'll be damned," Simon said.

"And another thing," McKee went on, "someone else was looking for Guiseppe today."

"Oh, who?"

"An Irishman called Eamon O'Beirne. I think that's how you pronounce it. Anyway, he wrote it down for me. Here it is." He passed over another slip of paper.

"Who the hell is he?" Simon said. "And how did he find you?"

"Down by the port. I was looking after the engine in one of my boats. Someone had sent him to me. He told me he was an expert on illuminated manuscripts and then seemed as if he wished he hadn't. As if I cared. I don't know what illuminated manuscripts are."

"I'm not sure I do," Simon said. "Do you, Richard?"

"More or less, but this gets odder and odder."

"I'll tell you another thing," McKee went on. "I think he was frightened. I've seen a lot of frightened people and I know the signs."

"I expect most of us who grew up when we did have been frightened ourselves," Simon said. "Well, thanks, McKee, for all you've done, though who or what Mr. O'Beirne is I don't know, I'm sure."

44

McKee had another drink and then pushed off in his Gordini. Simon and I looked at each other. "I don't know about Mr. O'Beirne, either," I said to him, "but those letters came from your solicitor or ex-solicitor in Ireland. O'Beirne is scarcely a good old native English name. Shanks, as he likes to call himself, was in Ireland during the war. I think someone ought to go and have a chat with that solicitor. It's obvious you can't. You've got to hold the fort here. I'll go."

"It's damn decent of you, Richard, but I don't see why . . ."

"I was almost killed yesterday, too, remember. "I've a stake in this now. Quite a personal one. What's this solicitor chap like?"

"Manahan? I've had very few dealings with him really. A bit on the smooth side, I always thought. All right, Richard, I'll call him and tell him you're coming. What about a seat on the airplane?"

"If you'll lend me a car I'll go into Ajaccio and badger Air France."

"Yes. O.K. Take it."

I left him at the telephone. I didn't feel particularly good about deceiving him, but there was little else I could do. Obviously I had to see Deforge to tell him what had happened, and to see if it was safe for me to visit Ireland or whether I'd be clapped in jail because of the irregularities on my passport.

In Ajaccio I went into a hotel on the Cours Napoleon. The telephone was in a hot little room at the back. I got through almost immediately.

"It's rather too warm for me," I said. "I thought in July the temperature was seldom as high."

"You are correct. But this is an exceptional year. Where are you?"

"In the Hotel Epinard."

"I see. Can anyone hear you?"

"I don't think so. I'm sweltering in a tiny room. A man called Shanks wants the place. Do you know that?"

"Yes. What else?"

"Quite a lot. I think I should see you. And I want a ticket on a plane."

"Where to?"

"Dublin."

"I see. Come to Rodeo Beach in an hour's time. Swim out to sea." There was a click as he hung up.

Rodeo Beach was a small and charming crescent of sand off the road which leads to the Isles Sanguinaires.

I rented a key and a cabin from an old lady beside the steps, changed my clothes, and walked out into the sea. It was warm and clear and clean. Yachts dotted the vast expanse of blue water in front of me. Across the great bay tier upon tier of mountains backed up against the sky. A military jet came slanting in over one of them in that thrusting, purposeful, slightly sinister way they have.

Suddenly a head bobbed up alongside me. It was Deforge. He looked very much at home in the sea. As he turned on his back the water dripped from the shoulders burned dark by the sun.

"Well?" he said.

"There's an Irish solicitor called Manahan," I told him. "He may be behind the whole thing. He's up to his neck in it anyway, I'm pretty sure, and I want to go and have a chat with him. Am I clear?"

"Yes, there should be no trouble."

"There's someone called O'Beirne, an Irishman, floating around here too, making inquiries. Do you know anything about him?"

He frowned. "O'Beirne? No. Another Irishman. That is interesting."

"I think so too. What about McKee?"

He smiled. "McKee is an adventurer," he said, "but not a political one. He is only interested in money."

"They sometimes go together. What about the ticket?"

He put his hand down to the waistband of his shorts and pulled up a small package in waterproof wrapping. "Here it is," he said. "You find the meeting place unusual?" he went

46

on, as I took it. "I prefer it to one on land. It is safer. The sea keeps its secrets."

He turned away from me and began to swim a long steady crawl out toward the glittering center of the bay. Perhaps he wasn't such a bad agent after all.

6

Legal Aid

Next morning I caught an Air France Caravelle out of Ajaccio. I changed at Orly and was in Dublin about teatime. My London club has one of those interchange arrangements with its opposite number in Dublin. I took a taxi to it and gave my name to the hall porter and the secretary. When I had washed and changed after the journey I wandered along toward the reading room with the intention of killing the evening as best I could.

The first person I saw was Roddy Marston, Sue's brother. He was sitting in an armchair reading *Sporting Life*.

"Dr. Livingstone, I presume?" he said, looking up and seeing me. "Where have you been lately? George Verschoyle told me you'd sold up your horses and gotten out of racing. Is it true?"

"Absolutely," I answered. "I've been staying with your sister and Simon in Corsica."

"Oh, still together, are they? How she sticks with that man I can't understand." Roddy and Sue had had one of those very close brother and sister relationships you sometimes come across, usually in the children of elderly and indigent parents such as theirs had been. It was no secret that Simon and Roddy had never hit it off, though I always thought the dislike they pro-

48

fessed for each other was exaggerated and founded in some odd way on a kind of mutual respect. But Roddy's book on the duration of the marriage must have been a losing one, which cannot have helped. He was a cheerful young ruffian and a much better amateur rider than I had ever been, and I always enjoyed his company.

"Not only together but flourishing," I said, rubbing salt into the wound. "What are you doing here anyway? Horsecoping?"

"No. It's a bloody funny thing, Richard. There's a new race, a thousand-pound amateur hurdle at Malloran Park tomorrow. I was called a day or two back and offered a ride in it. I don't know the woman who owns the thing and I hardly know Bellfort, who trains it either."

"What it is to be famous," I said. "Nothing like that used to happen to me when I was riding. Has it a chance?"

"It's a horse called Ready Token. Bellfort said the chap who rides for him over here was down with summer flu and all the other passable Irish amateurs were booked. According to the form book it has a hell of a chance. That's why I said I'd come. I haven't been on a horse since our season stopped, but I didn't see any reason to tell him that."

I also guessed that there was a substantial present in the offing. Roddy was permanently short of money. How he continued to persuade the stewards to go on allowing him to ride as an amateur was a source of considerable bewilderment to his friends. It has been said of him in fact by some kind of acquaintance that he feared no one on, under, or over the Turf save the Stewards of the National Hunt Committee.

"Who owns him?" I asked.

"The Contessa di Maggiore, if you please."

"Does she indeed? And who may she be? I don't seem to remember her in racing."

"She's only just come into it. This is her first horse. Bellfort bought it for her. Naturally enough he's anxious to do well for her and keep her in the riding game. Which is why, no doubt," he added with becoming modesty, "they've asked me to ride."

49

"Quite so. But, look, you do come over a fair amount, spotting horses and one thing or another, don't you?"

"By and large I suppose I do."

"Did you ever come across a solicitor called Manahan?"

"Charles Coningsby Manahan? Of course I did."

"Why of course?"

"Because he's into everything. A very smooth operator indeed, if you ask me. He goes racing on and off, mostly around here or at the Curragh. Doesn't know anything about it, but takes damn good care to mix with the chaps whom he can buy stud farms for. He has all the right answers and all the right contacts. He'll buy you a house or a horse or a cut into a company at the drop of a hat. But I'm dining with these owners of mine, I'd better be off." He lounged out.

I picked up *Sporting Life*. Our Irish correspondent referred to tomorrow's race as attracting a great deal of interest and was of the opinion that Ready Token represented a sound each way wager, especially since he would lack no assistance from the saddle, that leading English amateur, Mr. R. Marston, having accepted the ride. I wondered if he would be quite so confident if he knew that Mr. R. Marston had not been on a horse for a month.

After that I had a solitary dinner in the nearly empty club dining room, drank a glass of port with an elderly member, and went to bed, considerably interested in the fact that Shanks' house guest, the so-charming Contessa di Maggiore, was running a horse tomorrow and that Sue's brother was to ride it.

At ten-thirty the next morning I presented myself at the offices of Messrs. Kendrew, McKintosh and Manahan, solicitors.

After the manner of modern solicitors' offices, this one had been considerably spruced up. There were thick carpets on the stairs and passages, a waiting room with an antique table, Jack Yeats pictures on the walls, and plenty of the best slick magazines to look at while you thought about making your will or saving your skin or beggaring your neighbor, or whatever you do think about in solicitors' waiting rooms.

50

Mr. Manahan's office, when I got there, conformed to type. There was about an acre of red plush carpet, two Georgian windows with a desk between them, comfortable armchairs, and not a paper to be seen, even on the desk, which was graced only by a tooled leather pen set.

Charles Coningsby Manahan went with the room. He had a young-old face, very carefully tended hair going fashionably gray at the temples, a pinstripe suit, and a cutaway collar. He looked more like an advertisement for men of distinction than a solicitor. I suppose it wasn't his fault, but I didn't like either him or the setup. I don't see why solicitors' offices should look like Harley Street consulting rooms even if you often come out of them feeling much the same. There were two Lionel Edwards water-colors on the walls, just to show Mr. Manahan was a good sport, I suppose. One of them was of the Ward Union Staghounds with a chap in the foreground falling into a large, dirty ditch. I wondered if Mr. Manahan had ever fallen into a large, dirty ditch. I doubted it.

He shook me warmly by the hand and asked me to sit down. Then he inquired after the health of Simon Herald and his charming wife. "He can't get over himself, I gather," he said.

"No," I answered. "And he has asked me, in very general terms, of course, to act for him."

"I see. Well, you realize that the clients I represent are prepared to make an offer—a very handsome offer—for Simon's Corsican property?"

"Yes, I've read the correspondence. Just what is the offer in figures?"

"Well, subject to title, of course—but I've no doubt that that's in order and that Simon had it looked into carefully when he bought the place—we are prepared to offer . . ." He named a sum which almost raised the hair on my head.

"Look," I said, "have you found uranium there?"

He gave one of those careful, professional laughs. "No," he said. "It's not quite as romantic as that. I will be candid with you, Mr. Graham. I am acting for an international consortium

51

which has its headquarters in Ireland. They wish to develop that portion of the coast. Simon's property is slap in the middle of it."

He wasn't being candid with me. It was a good story, but I didn't believe a word of it. International developers didn't try killing for business purposes.

"Well," I said, "I'm afraid I can't give you any encouragement. He won't sell. That's the long and the short of it. It's too bad for your clients, but he just doesn't want the money."

"He's insane if he doesn't sell at that price." He looked at me with something approaching commiseration.

"Perhaps. But the message I've been asked to give you is that under no circumstances and at no price will he agree. And please don't bother him with any more offers."

He opened his mouth to say something when the desk buzzer sounded. Reaching forward he flipped a switch.

"The Contessa di Maggiore is waiting, Mr. Manahan," the tinny disembodied voice of the secretary said. "She asked me to tell you . . ."

He grabbed for the telephone attachment to cut out the voice-to-voice connection. Putting it to his ear he listened intently for a moment or two. I was clearly not intended to hear what was being said, which was natural enough in a solicitor's office. "Very well. I'll be ready right away." Turning to me as he replaced the receiver, he put on a practiced smile. "Do forgive me for that interruption," he said. "I've been reminded that I have another appointment almost immediately. The answer, then, that we must tell our people, is a very definite no?"

"Yes, I'm afraid so."

"Very well then." He half-rose in his chair.

"Just before I go, Mr. Manahan," I said, drawing a bow at a very wild venture, "do you happen to know someone from Dublin called Eamon O'Beirne?"

He sat down again with a thump. Some flicker of expression showed in his eyes for a second. It might have been wariness or it might have been fear, but whatever it was it only lasted an instant. Then his professional control took over and it was gone.

52

"Eamon O'Beirne," he repeated. "Eamon O'Beirne. Of course. I have it now. Everyone in Dublin knows everyone else, you know, Mr. Graham, at least after a fashion. He is an expert, *the* expert I believe, on illuminated manuscripts and on writing them or whatever you do. He moves very much in the writing and television worlds around here. But why do you ask?"

"Because," I said slowly, "he is in Corsica now. And he has been inquiring about a lake on Simon Herald's grounds. Can you imagine why he should be doing that? Has he any connection with your clients?"

There was no doubt about it at all; I had scored some sort of a hit. He was alert and watchful underneath the veneer of charm and smoothness. "No," he said slowly, "I can assure you of that. He has not."

As I went out I glanced into the waiting room. An extraordinarily smartly dressed woman was sitting reading *Country Life,* and as shapely a pair of legs as I have ever seen were crossed beneath her short tight skirt. The foot on the floor was tapping up and down as if in impatience. Controlled blonde curls crept out from under a cute little hat. A pair of those enormous circular dark glasses covered the upper part of her face. I got the feeling that I had seen her before. I felt that feeling was coming to me rather too often, though in the case of Shanks it had been justified. I put it out of my mind—or tried to—and went down to the street.

7

Ready Token

The Contessa di Maggiore—whom I thought I had seen before —was an important and urgent client of Mr. Manahan's. Her horse was running that afternoon and Roddy Marston had been sent for to ride it. Mr. Manahan was acting for whoever wanted Simon's property, and he had been, to say the least of it, more than mildly interested when I mentioned that Eamon O'Beirne was in Corsica. It was all too intriguing a combination of circumstances to be entirely accidental. I decided that I, too, would pay a visit to the Malloran Park races that afternoon.

It didn't take long to hire a car and to inquire the way. It was about a two-hour journey from Dublin, they told me, and off I went.

The roar of the track brought back vivid memories to me. I felt that familiar tingle of excitement run through me as it does, I suppose, through any man who has ever owned or ridden race-horses when he hears this roar and sees the green ribbon of turf, the white rails, and the black fences spread out before him. I have always felt that when an old hunter's ears go forward the moment he sees or hears hounds he is experiencing the same feeling. Yet it was with a slight sensation of being out of it all that I avoided the trainers' and jockeys' gate and paid my way in.

54

Roddy's race was third on the list. I walked down to the parade ring, partly to look at the horses and partly to see if I could find anyone I knew, especially George Verschoyle, who had trained for me and who often came over at this time of year to look out for something useful. The first race was a maiden hurdle and the runners were a pretty undistinguished-looking lot. I circulated slowly around the tree-shaded ring, and in a few minutes came on George. He was deep in conversation with one of the leading Irish trainers who, in common with most of the top trainers in that country, look and dress more like well-to-do doctors or businessmen than horsy types. This particular one had a bedside manner too, and, judging by some of his owners, he probably needed it.

After a few minutes George caught my eye. "Good God," he said when he came over to me. "I thought you were abroad. What are you doing here? Don't tell me you're getting back into racing without letting me know?"

"No," I said, "I'm not. I suppose you're looking for something to stock up for the winter?"

"That's about it. But the ruddy prices they're asking! It gets worse all the time."

"Then I don't suppose I could get back even if I wanted to. Look, George, there's something odd going on which concerns a friend of mine. I think a Dublin solicitor called Manahan is mixed up in it. I hear he races a bit. Did you ever come across him?"

"No, but I've heard of him all right. Everyone here has. Takes you racing in his box in the Curragh which gets put down as office expenses and asks for your business at the same time. You probably know the type. And now I come to think of it, I believe he isn't Irish at all."

"What!"

"Well, one of his colleagues—they all hate his guts by the way—told me once, when there was some racing law case going on in which Manahan was involved, that he'd gotten himself invalided out of the army during the war, had come over here, taken his exams, and bought the practice."

"Do you remember Hamley-Richardson?"

"Man who won the National twice just before the war? Yes, of course, but he's been off the Turf a long time now."

"I know, but he did much the same thing. Came over here during the war and made a lot of money. I wonder if there could be any link up between them."

"Blessed if I know. Look, they're going out and there's a chap I particularly want to see. The best place to watch from, by the way, is the stand down by the last fence."

I didn't really concentrate very much on the racing until Roddy's hurdle came around. I was trying to figure out what sort of a racket we'd all gotten ourselves mixed up in and making no sense of it at all. Then I walked over and secured a good place on the rails of the parade ring.

Ready Token was a slashing great bay horse by Archive. The punters were going for him like hell and he was a firm favorite at even money in a field of twenty. I remembered what Roddy had said about his own condition and refrained from betting. The Contessa looked extremely decorative in the ring and still wore her large dark glasses. Her racing colors, I noticed with a quickening of interest, were claret with a white sash.

The first time past the stands it was obvious that Ready Token was taking a hell of a hold. Roddy had him tucked in on the rails with four in front of him, but he didn't look as if he was enjoying himself one bit. I wondered what would happen if and when the leading horses weakened. There was quite a hill up to the finish.

Three hurdles out they did weaken. Two of them dropped back beat and a wide gap opened on the rails. Ready Token shot to the front. It was far too soon to my way of thinking. I hoped he was fitter than his rider.

They were still in front over the last, but two others were closing the gap fast. Ready Token would want to pull out something extra if he was to win, and he'd have to do it by himself, for his rider was no help to him at all.

Roddy, who was no fool once he got on a horse, had sense

enough to sit still, or as still as he could in his condition. Then from somewhere he pulled out enough strength to get at the horse with his hands. Ready Token lengthened his stride. He just lasted home by a neck. He must have been a good horse.

I went to see the unsaddling. As he stripped the horse Roddy caught my eye, gave me a broad wink, and walked into the weighing room. I waited for him. I thought there might be celebrations and I thought I'd like an introduction to the Contessa.

It was not long before Roddy was changed and out again. "Did you ever in your life see anything like that?" he asked me.

"No," I said truthfully, "I didn't."

"I suppose if I'd been fit I'd have had almost twenty pounds in hand. Christ, he takes a hold. I just gave up. There was nothing I could do but try and stay there. I thought the post would never come. Let's have a drink. I'm aching all over."

"Where's the owner?"

"Gone back to Dublin. I'm to rendezvous at the Russell, if she doesn't change her mind. Anyway, I'll take damn good care the present is all right."

We had a couple of drinks and watched the rest of the racing. I met a few more old friends and, after the last race, had some more drinks. Time passed quickly as it does on these occasions, and when I got out to my car most of the crowd had gone.

As I was putting the key into the door a youngish chap approached me and asked me if I was going to Dublin. I said I was.

"I wonder if you'd mind giving me a lift, sir?" he said. "I had a win on the last and by the time I'd collected and had a drink or two I found I'd missed my bus."

In a way it was much what I'd been doing myself and I felt sympathetic. Part of my mind also was busy thinking how I could get in on the Contessa's party at the Russell. I told him I'd take him.

We drove through Malloran village and out onto the main Carlow-Dublin road. I suppose we'd gone about ten miles when he reached under his coat as if for a cigarette.

He didn't take out a cigarette case. What he did take out was a small stubby belly gun from one of those waist holsters which make them so difficult to spot. He pointed it at me with what looked like a practiced hand. "There is a turn to the left half a mile further on," he said. "Take it."

8

Who Sups with the Devil

"You know," I said, pressing my foot a little harder on the accelerator, "guns are funny things. You've either got to use them or they're only pieces of metal. And if you shoot me now we'll both go into the ditch. I can't imagine you want that."

"You have about half a minute to make up your mind," he answered coolly. "I expect I know as much about guns as you do. I shall shoot you through the hand. It'll give me just enough time to grab the wheel and keep her steady. Your hand will be quite a mess and I don't think you'll put up much fight. If we bother to get you to a doctor we can always say you had an unfortunate accident with a sporting rifle. You don't want a crippled hand, do you? Here is the turn."

I glanced sideways at him. His mouth was set in a hard line. He had practically no lips at all. He didn't look in the least like the pleasant sort of chap I thought I'd picked up. I slowed down and took the turn.

We went along a side road for a mile or so and then, at his direction, through a large, ornate, pillared gateway. A steep, winding drive took us up toward the towers of a Victorian-Gothic mansion. I parked the car in the forecourt.

He told me to get out and, keeping just far enough away from me so that I couldn't get at him, marched me toward the house. He wasn't taking any chances with me, I noticed. As a matter of fact I didn't particularly want to get away just then. I was anxious to know just whom I was going to meet inside and who was so eager for my company that they had to send a gunman to get me.

We went into a vast hall carved and paneled and hideous, then up a thickly carpeted stone staircase and down a long passage. I noticed display cabinets of china, pictures in great gilt frames, Gothic chairs and chests, even a suit of armor, fully set up. I thought that I wasn't going to like the house, whatever my feelings about the inhabitants.

The man opened an arched door, heavy and ponderous, and ushered me into a room. It was one of those long, narrow, badly proportioned rooms which preponderate in Victorian-Gothic houses. It had been done over by a decorator and made as comfortable as could be. The original furniture had been replaced by good Georgian pieces. Tall, mullioned windows at one end looked out over a formal garden, and I could see the green of a lawn beyond.

Sitting at a table with a tray of drinks on it was Mr. Charles Coningsby Manahan, solicitor. He dismissed my escort with a wave of his hand.

"Nice to see you again, my dear chap," he said. "Care for a drink? Whiskey, vodka, gin?"

"I've had several already," I said. "But, seeing the circumstances, I don't suppose another will do me any harm. Scotch and soda, please."

He poured me the drink and held out a cigarette box.

"You're taking a hell of a chance, aren't you?" I said. "What if I write in to the Law Society and complain that you had me brought here at the point of a gun?"

"Of course you can do that if you like, but I don't really think it will do you much good. The letter will be sent on to me. I shall explain that you came entirely under your own free will and appear to be suffering from delusions."

60

"And if I press it?"

"Well, let me make it clear in the first place that the president and the two vice-presidents are all personal friends of mine. I entertain them frequently. But if you do, I suppose it is just possible that I might be required to swear an affidavit which will be no trouble to me and which will be believed, I assure you. After that, you will be ordered to pay the costs of the matter."

"I see. It was just a passing thought. I don't intend to complain anyway. Now, what do you want?"

"My clients want Simon Herald's land, Graham, and I'm afraid they intend to get it."

"Is it worth while asking why?"

"No. But I am empowered to offer you, personally, a very considerable sum of money if you can swing the deal."

"Fortunately, just at the moment, I don't want money."

"I was rather afraid of that. It seemed, however, worth trying once you were over here. And, I may add, it has been my experience that every man has his price."

"I would expect so from what I've heard of you. Perhaps I have too—in a way. Give me back ten years and the feeling that I have two spare necks in my pocket so that I could go back to riding over fences again. But I rather think that's beyond even your clients' powers."

"Unfortunately I don't act for the Almighty, though some of my clients appear to be under the illusion that I do. Well, then, let us abandon that approach for the moment and explore another. I understand Herald's wife is exceedingly fond of her brother."

"Yes."

"Young Marston is a reckless devil. He is also perennially short of cash."

"You seem to know a lot about him."

"I've made it my business to. At about this time in the Russell Hotel he is being given a very handsome check for his services this afternoon as an amateur jockey."

I put my glass down on the table. What a double-distilled fool

Roddy was, I thought. Why couldn't he take a gold watch and pawn it, but a check!

"Exactly," went on Manahan. "I see you follow me. If that check is placed before the stewards, I believe Marston will be in some trouble. Are you prepared to advise Susan Herald to use her influence with her husband to sell, provided we withhold the check?"

I thought about it. Manahan leaned back in his chair, alternatively sipping his drink and staring at the ceiling.

Sue and Roddy were very close, about as close as brother and sister could be. But Sue was in love with Simon. Given the facts, would she use her influence with him? I doubted it. Even if she did, I further doubted if it would do any good. They had misjudged their man. Basically I felt that, knowing Simon, nothing would move him now. He was in a fight and once in he was not the sort to pull out for anyone or anything.

"I don't think you know the man you're dealing with," I said. "If you step up the pressure on him, he's liable to start taking things—and people—apart." He was also, I reflected, liable to break up his own marriage and to run headlong into trouble, which was maybe what they wanted.

"Perhaps he, and you too, have underestimated who you are dealing with," Manahan answered. "If Marston's threatened downfall—and Herald's wife will certainly hear about it even if you don't tell her—does not influence him, then it is possible, I'm afraid, that there may be an executor's sale."

"I see. You put it very nicely. They'll kill him. Oh, I don't doubt it will be well dressed up as an accident and all that, but in the end that's what you really mean. Well, a lot of people tried in the war and he's still around. Come to think of it someone tried to do all of us in the other day and here I am too—largely due to Simon."

What the hell, I wondered, was in that lake, or was it the lake at all that held the secret? I also thought that I might be able to reach Manahan quickly enough to knock him out, get through the door, and make for Dublin before they raised the alarm. It was a remote chance, but if I could stop Roddy cashing that check at least one danger was eliminated. I got to my feet as aimlessly as I could. I measured the distance between Manahan and me. Then I raised myself on my toes. At that moment the door behind me opened.

"Ah, my dear," Manahan said, getting to his feet himself.

I turned. It was the Contessa. She was still wearing the clothes I had seen her in at the races and also those infernal dark glasses.

"I'm afraid Mr. Graham is intransigent, my dear," Manahan said, after he had introduced us. "He also, unless I am very much mistaken, was contemplating an assault upon my person, inflicting actual bodily harm just before you came in." He chuckled. "Another drink, Graham? You may need one." He poured it without waiting for my acceptance and set the glass down on the chimney-piece some distance from me. "If I may quote an adage," he went on, looking at the glass and then at me, "who sups with the devil should use a long spoon."

"That's something I should think you'd know all about," I said sourly. "How in hell did you get mixed up in all this, whatever it is, Manahan?"

He laughed again. "A fondness for money, let us say, and comfort and a certain absence of scruples. Otherwise I might have had to dip into my clients' accounts, a most sordid and silly proceeding I always think and one which is inevitably found out. And, don't misunderstand me, Graham, I enjoy living with the best and on the best, and I intend to keep it that way."

"I'm sure Mr. Graham knows O'Beirne was with us in Corsica for a while," the Contessa put in. "We're interested in him, Mr. Graham, very interested indeed. Perhaps you'd care to stay here for a little and tell us all about him."

She had a distinctive, curiously attractive voice. Again, I could have sworn I had heard it before. She had unwittingly given herself away by crediting me with more knowledge than in fact I had, when she assumed I knew that O'Beirne had been with them in Corsica. O'Beirne had been mixed up with them in some way. And now they thought O'Beirne and I were in cahoots. Very interesting.

63

"I suppose that's a threat," I said. "By the way, where are we?"

Manahan answered me. "Ballymere Stud," he said. "One of the enterprises in which my friend and client, Edgar Shanks, is a large stockholder. You have met Edgar, I believe. You know, I really think you should accept the Contessa's invitation, Graham."

"You're not seriously suggesting you can throw me into a dungeon and keep me there?"

"Well, no, not exactly. Dungeons *are* a little out of date." Manahan held his glass up to the light and examined its contents. "Let us take a purely hypothetical case. I'll put it to you this way: if, for instance, a guest in a country house were to fall ill; if the local doctor was fond of the bottle—too fond—and had put himself under certain obligations to the owner of the house for financial and other assistance at vital moments; if, and of course I insist all this is purely hypothetical, that same doctor was convinced that the house was filled with members of the International Set who sustained themselves solely with drink and drugs; if he'd had to treat a few cases of the sort before— it's quite extraordinary, you know, the number of people nowadays who cannot carry on without barbiturates—well, you get my meaning, I'm sure. Sedatives could and would, no doubt, be prescribed in large, indeed, massive doses. And if by any unfortunate chance the patient were to succumb, there would be no difficulty, no difficulty at all, about the signing of the death certificate. I'd also better make it quite clear, in case you aren't prepared to treat all this as a pure hypothesis, that during the next fortnight I personally shall be in the west of Ireland fishing."

"Not Corsica? The fishing there is excellent too, I'm told."

"I find dear old Ireland much more relaxing after the cares and worries of the modern professional life."

"You know, Manahan," I said, "I'm almost beginning to like you."

He chuckled. "May I inquire if you made your will or, as they quaintly refer to it over here, 'settled your affairs,' dear boy?

If not, and you feel the circumstances warrant it, I'd be happy to draw it up for you."

But I'd heard the door open behind me. Whoever came in was being very quiet and careful, but just not quite quiet enough. The thick carpet blanketed most of the sounds of his approach, but not all of them, as he must have thought it did.

They tell you nowadays that anything in your hand is a weapon. Even schoolgirls are taught to put pennies between their fingers as a knuckleduster for self-protection when walking home in the dark. That was all right with me. I had something in my hand. It all depended on the timing with which I used it. The man behind was very near now. Manahan was going on talking easily, jauntily, showing no signs of interest in anything save the drink in his hand.

"Myself as executor, with a power to charge costs, of course, I should suggest," I heard him saying.

I could almost feel the other man's breath. He was near enough. I spun on my toes and slung the whiskey into his eyes. It was the man who had held me up in my car. His hand was under his coat, feeling for his gun.

When the whiskey hit him he gave a yelp of pain. I slammed the glass at him. It was a cut-glass tumbler, good and tough and heavy. His fingers came out from under his jacket and groped up toward his face. I reached in and jerked out the gun. Getting him by the shoulder while he was still off-balance, I slammed him down on the sofa beside the Contessa. Then I pointed the gun in the general direction of the three of them. It was a 38 Smith and Wesson, as I saw when I had it in my hand. My thumb went over the hammer and pulled it back. It made a most satisfactory and threatening click.

"My sedatives have steel jackets on them," I said chattily to the room at large, "and leaden hearts and play for keeps."

"You really are a most violent sort of man," Manahan said. He was still leaning back in his chair and giving every indication of enjoying a quiet drink. He had plenty of nerve. No doubt in that practice of his, he needed it.

"Care to give me any legal advice now?" I asked him.

"Well, perhaps the old maxim *sic utere tuo ut alienum non laedas* would fill the bill. Shall I translate?"

"No thanks. Don't play Russian Roulette unless you know which chamber is empty. Will that do?"

"A little free, but it will pass."

"I'm going to suggest that you three play a sort of Russian Roulette now," I said. "In about ten seconds I'm going through that door. If the key is in the lock well and good, though I don't suppose it is. Half an hour's grace is what I want, and I intend to get it. I'm going to wait outside the door some of the time. If anyone of you comes out during that time, and this means you too, Contessa, you'll get a slug in your guts. I've no doubt that the accommodating doctor will treat you without any awkward questions. You can always explain it away as an accident with a sporting gun, as the hired help suggested to me in the car. It's your choice and your risk. After half an hour you should be safe. Unless, of course, I change my mind and decide to stay on a little longer. Good-bye."

"*Au revoir,* dear boy, for I fancy we shall meet again," Manahan said as I went.

There wasn't a key in the door. I hung around outside for a few minutes. Nobody called my bluff. I ran downstairs. The keys were still in my car. The room I'd just left was at the back of the house and the door was solid and thick. I doubt if anyone heard my going. I passed through the main gates of Ballymere Stud at fifty miles an hour, narrowly missed a boy on a bicycle who took to the ditch and some hens who didn't, and then went hell for leather back toward the main road.

This was fairly well signposted. I followed the posts to Dublin and at the first town I came to—I think it was Carlow—I stopped at a sign marked Hotel.

The girl behind the bar told me where the telephone was. Quite a few race-goers were still around drinking and talking, and as I passed a group of them on my way to the telephone I heard one of them say: "Stone cold certainty. That Marston doesn't come over here for nothing." As I opened the door of the booth, I wondered if he knew just how right he was.

I looked up the instructions for making long-distance calls in the telephone book and once I'd succeeded in getting through to the exhange, it took a surprisingly short time to reach the Russell Hotel. The desk said they would page Mr. Marston.

When Roddy did come to the phone he was, as I'd expected and dreaded, as high as a kite.

"Who is it?" he said. "Oh, Richard, it's you. I say, these people are dam' generous."

"I know," I told him grimly. "I've just been entertained by your Contessa."

"What! I wondered why she didn't turn up. This man she sent along doesn't know anything about racing, but he knows about buying drinks all right."

"Who is he?"

"Damned if I know, now you mention it. I believe he said he was some sort of assistant of Manahan's. Listen, Richard, I'd better go back. This party is just beginning to jump. I must say I don't go much for your snaking off with my lovely owner. You always were a one for the blind side of bed."

"Which side is that?" I snarled at him. "Sober up, will you? I want you to get out of there and to meet me at the airport. I suppose you still have the check?"

"What check? Oh, the one they gave me. Yes, of course. At least I hope so, unless I've lost the bloody thing."

"Well, don't cash it even if someone suggests that he'll do it for you tonight. You've walked into it, chum."

"What!"

"If you cash that check it'll be plonked on the senior steward's desk the moment it's cleared."

"Old Bosanquet! My God, why?"

"I can't explain it all now. But if it's any help to you, your charming lady friend has just tried to have me as her house guest at the point of a gun. I'm not at all sure, but I think she may have had the idea of murdering me into the bargain."

"Cripes! Times are tough all over."

"You can say that again. Am I getting through to you now or do I have to spell things out?"

"You're getting through all right. I am receiving you loud and clear. But what is this about? You *are* a chap for getting yourself mixed up in things. Wasn't there something . . ."

"Never mind about that. If I'm mixed up in anything this time, so are you and so is your sister. Now, will you try to make sense?"

"Sue? But, how the hell? Oh, all right, Richard. Go ahead. What is it?"

He was getting a bit sulky now. He was apt to get that way if he was crossed. It's an occupational disease of golden boys.

"Well, then, leave that party. Don't say you're meeting me. Go to the airport and try to get two seats on a night plane to London. I'll be there as soon as I can. I'm in some town or other. I think it's Carlow."

"I hope this adds up when you tell all, Richard. You're doing me out of a damn good party."

"I'm also saving your hide with old Bosanquet, chum. I don't think he's a fervent fan of yours at the best of times. Don't forget that."

I slammed down the receiver. "Like chimney sweepers come to dust," I said crossly as it lay in its cradle. I was out of patience with golden boys—and girls, too, for that matter, I reflected as I thought of the Contessa's neat blonde head. Sooner or later, I supposed, I would see her with those dark glasses off.

9

The Red Comes Up

But you couldn't remain out of patience with Roddy for very
long. I collected my bag from the club, left the car in the parking area, and found him waiting for me in the hall of the airport building.

"When is the plane?" I said.

"Now. We haven't got much time. I think you'd better get
yourself weighed in pretty quick."

It was a B.E.A. Vanguard and the flying time, we were told,
would be just under one hour.

"Have you got that check?" I asked him as we unfastened our
seat belts in the plane.

"Yes."

"Well, burn it."

"Listen, Richard, this would just about put me right with my
bank manager."

"Damn your bank manager. You can imagine, I suppose,
what the stewards will say when they see that check. Burn it." I
knew what money and Roddy were like. If I were to let up for
an instant he'd have second thoughts, take the money,
and chance the consequences.

With great reluctance he took a plain business envelope out of his pocket. It was unsealed and the check was inside. I snapped on my lighter and put it to the corner of the envelope. The flame licked the paper. A flicker of smoke crept around Roddy's fingers. The aircraft was half empty, which was just as well. Roddy crushed out the last remnants in an ash tray just as the steward bustled up.

"Really, gentlemen . . ."

"That's quite all right," Roddy said calmly. "I was just writing of a bad investment. Bring me two large brandies. My friend," he added, "will pay."

None of the seats around us was occupied, so when the drinks came, I told him as much as was good for him about what was going on. I also told him I intended to fly to Nice that night, if I could get a seat, and on to Corsica the following day.

He remained silent for a few minutes, and then he said, rather hesitantly for him, "Is this a private fight or can anyone join in?"

"What do you mean?"

"Well, I don't care much for being cheated and kicked around. I see now I was for the high jump if you hadn't caught up with me and that check. Racing is my life, after all. You'll understand that, Richard. I've nothing to do until August. I don't exactly expect the Contessa will be running after me to ride for her in Ireland again."

"Neither do I after that God awful performance you gave today."

He grinned and took another swig of brandy. "It wasn't very artistic was it? My hat, how they must have been sweating! I expect they were damn near as nervous as I was coming up the straight. I want to come along, Richard. I'm not much good with guns and things like you ex-glamor boys from the cloak-and-dagger days. But I could hold Sue's hand at moments, I suppose."

"Are you serious?"

"Of course I am. I suppose that bloody brother-in-law of mine will have me."

70

"I'll produce you as a surprise present. He can hardly kick you out."

Roddy might, I thought, be useful in whatever was brewing up, and he was certainly less likely to get us all into trouble if he was under our eyes rather than floating around foot-loose and fancy free, ready for anything and anybody. Moreover, I seemed to remember he was a very high-class lightweight boxer.

We were lucky in our connections that night. We just caught the Trident leaving for Nice. It carried us swiftly through the night sky high over the Alps to the south. I dozed the flight away as best I could, whilst Roddy drank more brandy and turned the pages of *Playboy*.

"Good job the Irish customs didn't catch you with that," I said, as I shifted my seat and caught him lusting over the charms of a bare and curvaceous female in full technicolor.

"I'm told by literary fellows that the stories in this magazine are of a very high standard."

"I noticed you were concentrating on the type," I said as I closed my eyes again.

We took a taxi to the Negresco and I booked two rooms. I was beginning to undress when he hammered on my door.

"What the hell now?" I asked him.

"Look, Richard, is there a casino still open at this time of night?"

"I think the Palais de Mediterrannée is, but they'll tell you downstairs."

"Lend me some French money, there's a good fellow, will you? I feel I'm in a groove, moneywise, tonight. Like to come along?"

"No."

I gave him what money I had or most of it, and climbed into bed. I was asleep in two minutes.

When I awoke next morning with the sun streaming across my windows and the traffic noises coming up, muted, from the Promenade des Anglais below, I felt fresh and well, which was more than I would had I gone out gambling with Roddy. Reaching for the telephone, I rang Air France and got two seats on

71

the after lunch Caravelle to Ajaccio. Then I put a call through to Simon. When he came on I told him what had happened and that I had Roddy with me.

"That infernal young horse-driver?" Simon said. "Why didn't you let him rot? Oh, well, I suppose we'll have to look after him and try to keep him out of mischief."

"You never know. He might be useful."

Simon snorted. "Useful for what? There aren't any horses around here. And he needn't think he's going to drive any of my cars. He's the worst person to let loose in charge of an internal combustion engine I've ever . . ."

I thought I'd better change the subject. "Look, Simon, where do you think I could get hold of McKee during the daytime?"

"I don't know. Somewhere down by the port, I suppose. O'Beirne found him there, didn't he?"

"Yes, I wonder if he knows where O'Beirne is now?"

"It's possible. He seems to know most things."

"I think I'll look for McKee this afternoon."

"O.K. I'll send a car for you. Want any help? Or are you taking Marston along?"

"God forbid. I'll leave him to you and his sister. I think I'll play this one alone, Simon."

Then I rang Deforge, but he was out on business. I was glad enough, for I really had nothing definite to tell him.

After that I told the floor waiter to bring me coffee and croissants. I was in the middle of breakfast when there was a thunderous knock on the door. It was, of course, Roddy.

"What did I say?" he announced happily, coming in and sitting on my bed. "Look, Richard, look. Lots and lots and *lots* of lovely money." He reached into his pocket and took out rolls and bundles of hundred-franc notes. "And that's not all," he said. "Here are some more." From another pocket he produced a fistful of notes of all sorts of denominations, loose this time. He threw them delightedly on to the counterpane and some fluttered to the floor. "I've more than made good that present," he went on. "At least I think I have. I don't really know what these things are worth."

I looked at the notes and leaned back dazedly. "You made it up all right," I said. "And with interest. Just how did you do it?"

"You play the black," Roddy said, picking some of the notes off the floor, "and the red comes up. I play the black and the black comes up. Zero, zero, zero—that's how I started off. Thought I might do worse than gamble on my nonexistent bank balance. After that I couldn't do a thing wrong. They actually came to watch me. Everybody loved me, except the croupiers. They looked as if they'd like to throw me into the street."

"Have you been to bed?" I asked him.

"Come to think of it, old boy, I haven't. You're drinking coffee. Good God, you can't do that. Get on that phone, will you, and order a bottle, no, a magnum of champagne."

"There have been worse ideas," I said. "But a bottle will do. And this time you pay."

I dressed slowly, and after we'd finished the champagne we took a taxi to the airport where we lunched. Roddy's spirits showed no signs of flagging, and the steward on the Caravelle who offered him orange juice was indignantly sent off in search of something stronger.

As we came down the steps of the plane at Ajaccio Airport the heat beat up at us from the tarmac and the sun danced on the wavelets in the bay. We walked past a party of legionnaires in their white kepis lounging around a truck. The sergeant in charge looked at us curiously and said something to the man beside him.

"Bit hot, isn't it," Roddy said, mopping his forehead.

"You're going to roast in those tweeds," I told him. "Better get some lightweight clothes if you're thinking of staying. Perhaps Simon will lend you some."

Sue was waiting for us. "Roddy!" she exclaimed delightedly, running toward us.

"You have him," I told her smiling. "He's all yours from now on."

"The Renault is for you, Richard," she said to me. "Mario came in with the Land Rover and I've strict instructions either he or I am to drive."

"I shouldn't much care to let Roddy loose on Corsican roads, I must say," I told her, looking at her brother. Putting my bag in the back of the Land Rover, I walked across to where the Renault was parked.

"Where are you off to?" Roddy demanded.

"Going to look for a friend," I said. "You and Simon can spend a quiet afternoon together talking about old times."

I drove along the new road from the airport with the heat waves dancing off its surface. The great curving beach, with a few sun worshipers scattered about, was on my left. I went up the hill and around the corners and came to the wide, straight, mile-long Cours Napoleon, the main throughfare of Ajaccio. I was glad enough to be alone. I'd always been something of a solitary.

Simon, I remembered, had parked his car in the Place de Gaulle which lay at the far end of the Cours Napoleon and looked out over the other side of the huge Bay of Ajaccio. I left the Renault there, paid the attendant, and inquired the way to the port. Following his directions, I went across the square, down the short street beyond the traffic lights, and into the tree-lined Place Marshal Foch. They are very military-minded with their place names in Ajaccio. At the far end of the Place was the quayside with boats moored alongside and advertisements for trips and expeditions by vedette to the Isles Sanguinaires and elsewhere. There was also a poster advertising a race-meeting—Trot, Plat et Obstacle. I glanced at it. A spirited picture showed two jockeys wildly flailing their whips riding flat out over a rough-looking fence.

The date had passed, which was just as well. Roddy would undoubtedly have insisted on looking for a ride and then he would have been in real trouble. I thought it unlikely that the meeting was run under Rules of Racing.

Further down, a biggish cargo ship was unloading. Out in the bay a liner lay at anchor.

I turned to the left and strolled along the port. It was blisteringly hot and there weren't many people at the café tables that

74

lined the waterfront. I told myself I was a fool to have come at this hour, but I urgently wanted to find O'Beirne. After a bit I began to ask people if they knew McKee or had seen him.

The first chap I stopped, a sailor, denied all knowledge of him; the second, a sort of dwarfish dockrat, who I was sure would know his whereabouts if anyone did, looked frightened and sidled away; the third said he thought McKee was out of Ajaccio. By this time I'd reached the end of the port and was beginning to think I'd better give up and wait until evening, then I could go back to the *son et guitares* and wait for him there. The trouble was that at the back of my mind I had an idea that time was running out and I'd better find O'Beirne soon. When you've been mixed up in these sorts of affairs before and you get an idea like that you don't discard it lightly.

I turned and retraced my steps. The cafés were just as empty as when I walked down. There didn't seem much I could do. I thought I'd pick a place I liked where I could keep an eye on things and kill an hour or so over a drink. I was looking for somewhere suitable when a sudden step sounded behind me and my arm was gripped.

I don't like sudden steps and people who grip my arm from behind, especially in circumstances such as these. I tensed my muscles.

"No, Mr. Graham, not here," a heavy voice said with a hint of amusement. "You were looking for me, sir."

I turned. It was McKee, all right. He was almost on top of me. Seen standing up, he looked like a very big man.

"Yes," I said, "I was. News travels fast here, I see."

"Some news, sir." There was a hint of mockery in his constant deference. I thought I'd noticed it the night we met him. I was sure of it now. "Shall we go and have a drink, sir? Somewhere cool where we can talk?"

Without waiting for an answer he led me past empty tables into the dark interior of a café very near where we'd been standing. A mahogany bar ran down one side of the room. There was a tiled floor, a banquette seat divided into partitions along the

75

wall opposite the bar, and some more tables with marble tops in front of it. McKee went on toward the back, banging twice with his fist on the bar as he passed.

At the very end of the room there were two booths. These had hollow benches of some dark polished wood and porthole windows high up in the walls to light them. McKee pushed himself into a corner of one of the benches. I sat opposite him. His bulk seemed to fill the little booth.

A man in a striped apron appeared with two glasses of pastis and a jug of water on a tray. He put them on the table between us. After the sunlight outside it was quite dark in here. Taking out a package of cigarettes, McKee offered me one. A spurt of flame from the match lit up his heavy features. He was looking impassively at me.

"Another of my offices," he said. "'You can talk as you like here. Just what do you want, Mr. Graham?"

"I want to know where to find Eamon O'Beirne," I said.

"Everyone, especially if they're English, thinks I know everything around here," he said evasively.

"Well, you do more or less, don't you? O'Beirne came to you. Has he been back?"

He glanced, almost furtively I thought, at the watch on his wrist. "Oh, yes, he's back all right."

"What for?"

"Now, if *you* had any business with me, Mr. Graham, you wouldn't like me to tell it around, would you?"

"That depends on the business. I could make this worth your while."

Again he shot a glance at his watch. He sipped his drink, put it down, and gazed at me. In the gloom his heavy face was expressionless. "If your proposition was worthwhile it might change things," he said. "How much?"

"What's it worth? I don't know the going rate around here."

"Let's say twenty pounds—in English notes."

"That seems a bit steep for a couple of questions and one answer. The going rate seems to run high around here. Let's say a tenner."

76

"Ten pounds! Mr. Graham, would you sell a man's secrets for ten pounds?" Again, somewhere behind those heavy features I sensed he was laughing at me.

"I don't know what the current exchange for thirty pieces of silver is," I said. "Fifteen, then, and a little more information thrown in for luck." I took three crisp Bank of England five-pound notes from my wallet and laid them on the table in front of me.

"Such as?"

"Such as what he looks like, how I'll recognize him when I catch up with him."

"The address is 20 Rue Trianon. You go past the Plat d'Or and turn to the left. He's youngish, early thirties, maybe. Doesn't look like my idea of a scholar."

"A lot of them don't nowadays. What does he look like?"

"More of an athlete, sort of, as if he'd done a bit of boxing in his time. Broad-shouldered, small head, clean-shaven. Fit sort of chap. Likes walking and climbing—and diving, too, he told me."

"I see. What did he come back to you for?"

"Well, now, that's an interesting one, Mr. Graham. He wanted to find out anything he could about Mr. Herald's house. How many people there were in it, servants included—That sort of thing. Wanted to know what Mr. Herald was like. I told him I thought he was fairly tough. I wonder would I have been right, Mr. Graham?"

"You might, at that." I pushed the money across the table and got to my feet.

He picked up the notes and tucked them away. "Another piece of information for you," he said, "and for free this time."

"What?"

"You're not the only person who has been looking for O'Beirne today."

"Oh," I said as casually as I could.

"There have been two of them. I knew the first."

"Did you tell him anything?"

"No, Mr. Graham. He didn't treat me nice and handsome like

you did. He tried the heavy with me. I don't go so much for being pushed around, Mr. Graham."

"I should think you mightn't. Who was he?"

"A Foreign Legion Colonel from Bonifacio. Name of Gregorov. He's a fairly rough hombre, Mr. Graham."

"I see. And the other?"

His heavy features creased into a frown. "That's just the trouble," he said, "that's what I don't know. It was a boy, a damned tousle-headed boy."

10

The Col de Sorba

I hurried toward the Rue Trianon, my mind racing. I hoped I'd be in time. I didn't know what McKee was up to, but I hadn't liked the way he'd kept looking at his watch. And I thought now that I knew pretty well who the tousle-headed boy was.

The Rue Trianon was a narrow, unfrequented street where the sun didn't seem able to penetrate. Tall, shabby houses, the plaster peeling from them in large patches, their wooden shutters unpainted and rickety, leaned toward each other shutting out the light.

The street numbers appeared to begin at the end farthest away from me. The house next to me was 44. Some of the numerals had gone from the doors. I went along slowly, counting the odd and even numbers as I passed.

I came opposite Number 20 and stopped. As I did so someone stepped out of its doorway. He glanced quickly up and down the street. I bent down and began to tie a nonexistent shoelace. I heard his feet on the pavement going away from me. I straightened up. Even from the back there was no mistaking the small head and boxer's shoulders. It was O'Beirne, all right.

Slung carelessly over one of his shoulders was a hiker's knapsack. As I watched, he hitched it up. One of the flap pockets had been carelessly tied down. Sticking out beneath it I could see part of a snorkel mask and diving equipment.

I followed him. At the end of the street he turned right and then crossed the Cours Grandval. He went down the long slope to the Place de Gaulle and I followed him at a distance. In the Place he walked straight to where a green Simca was parked. Unlocking it he threw the knapsack into the back, tipped the attendant and pulled into the one-way traffic. I ran to the Renault.

He drove around the Place to the traffic lights on the Cours Napoleon. I hadn't much trouble keeping him in sight. He crossed when the lights changed and went on down the long street. There were two more traffic lights and at one of them I almost lost him, just catching the very end of the green. He headed out toward the airport and then, at the entrance to the town where the main junction is, he took the road for Bastia.

He was bucketing along fairly fast. Except for the traffic lights, I hadn't had much trouble tailing him in town. But once in the country it was a different matter.

The road ran through fertile lowlands beside a river. It was virtually empty of traffic. I assumed that O'Beirne, if he wasn't a bigger bloody fool than I took him for, would keep an eye on his driving mirror. I had to stay far enough behind to avoid suspicion and near enough not to lose him. I also had to keep an eye on my own mirror. What game McKee was playing I didn't know, but it seemed a fair assumption that he might decide to have me followed. However, after a while, and when absolutely nothing showed up behind me, I began to give more and more attention to the car in front.

O'Beirne was pushing on. That made it easier for me and less likely that he would have time to watch what was happening behind him. Pretty soon the road began to climb steeply in a succession of almost Alpine corners. It had recently been re-engineered, widened and rebuilt, but, even so, one had to keep one's wits to get up it at any speed. I noticed disused bits of the old road as we passed, and reflected that trying to make time

80

on its narrow serpentine surface must have been hell. O'Beirne was following the technique of many Corsican drivers in keeping his hand all but permanently on the horn. That helped me to assess the distance between us and to adjust my speed if I thought he was coming nearer or drawing away.

Eventually we swung across the head of the pass where an old ruined castle kept permanent sentry. My mirror showed a breathtaking view behind me, but I hadn't time to enjoy it. A wide tarmac road led us through a pine forest, the great trees towering up along the foothills of the mountains. After about a mile there was a banner across the road proclaiming HOTEL DU MONTE D'ORO, and on the right was a long low inn built of wood and comfortable-looking.

The green Simca was well ahead of me now, and I had little option but to let him go. It's a difficult job to tail a car along a road you don't know, as I have found out before. Wide curves banked and bordered with low white walls climbed up through the forest. I put on a bit of speed. Almost anywhere here he might pull aside and lose me. But after a couple of miles I caught a flash of sun on green and saw the little car high up in front of me. I now realized I'd given away more distance than I should and I pressed on. It was just as well that I did.

Suddenly I shot out of the forest onto a steep descent. Huge, snowclad peaks were all around. In front, the road seemed to hang over a valley hundreds of feet below. The mountains formed a great circle of which I was on the very edge. To my right a road ran back and upward along the side of a ridge. A signpost said COL DE SORBA. O'Beirne and the Simca had disappeared.

Slamming on the brakes, I pulled up and got out. The landscape was empty of human habitation. The sun beat down out of a cloudless sky. A faint wind lifted the boughs of the scattered pines. I ran to the edge where the two roads met. Below was nothingness; to my left steep hairpins went downward; to the right was the road leading to the Col. And then I saw him halfway up the road to the Col, just rounding a corner and climbing hard. There was a glimpse of the green car and then he was gone, to reappear again in an instant on the short straight stretch before another corner.

I had the Renault after him as soon as I could get her into gear. The first few hundred yards were straight enough. I pushed her into third and made the engine scream. Then we were into the angles. The road was barely a car's width. On one side was the sheer, unguarded drop, on the other the mountain wall. I hoped nobody was thinking of coming down that day. But the chances I took on the bends were rewarded. Every now and then I caught glimpses of him above me, and each time he was nearer.

Then, all at once, I was running up to the crest. A sign said COL DE SORBA. ALT. 1305 M. From the top I could survey a long stretch of road as it dropped down the further side between sparse pines. He wasn't on it. I had lost him again.

I walked over to the marking post and took stock of the situation. High as I had now come, yet another range of snow-topped peaks reared up around me. On either side of the road the ground fell steeply away. There was nowhere here to hide a car. He wasn't in front of me, and he certainly wasn't behind me. And he hadn't been all that far away when he disappeared, for I had been gaining on him. Therefore, somewhere here he must have found a place to leave the road.

Locking the door I walked back the way I had come. Again the emptiness of the place struck me. Not a car appeared. Far down in the valley below me was a tiny village. Apart from that I was utterly alone in the high Alps of Corsica, alone with the snow and the sun and the tall pines. If O'Beirne wanted seclusion he couldn't have picked a better place.

A few hundred yards down the road I picked up the trail. Unless I had been searching for it I certainly wouldn't have come on it. Something that looked like the beginning of a track ran at an angle into the forest. Bending down I could just make out the bruising of tires on earth. Further in there were broken twigs, crushed leaves, and more marks where little ridges of earth had been crumbled by tires.

I followed, treading lightly. The path wound and curled

amongst the trees and skirted outcrops of rock. Some bird shrieked a shrill warning at me and fluttered away. I went on, ever more cautiously, scanning as best I could through the trees what lay beyond every turn before I took it.

Then, all of a sudden, I saw the back of the Simca. He had run it off the path into a sort of bay formed by a screen of scrub and maquis. It was empty. A few paces further on and I was at the edge of a little clearing. On the far side of this, right under the trees, was a log hut. It was very small indeed, with just a door, a window on either side, and a brick chimney. At one time it must have been the shelter of a forest ranger or a fire-guard. It looked dilapidated now; the roof needed repair and one of the windows was broken. But smoke was rising from the chimney. O'Beirne hadn't wasted much time.

I surveyed the hut, the clearing, and the silent surrounding forest for a minute or two. Then I took a deep breath and walked across the empty space.

The door was shut; there was a leather latch at shoulder height. Lifting my fist, I knocked on the wood with my knuckles.

A voice said in English without any preamble, "Come in."

An unpleasant feeling that perhaps I was expected took hold of me. I pulled down the latch. Putting my hand on the door I pushed it open. Then I stood stock still on the threshold.

Directly in front of me was a table. Behind the table O'Beirne was sitting. On it, propped on some cans and with his hand around the trigger, was one of those underwater harpoon guns. Its arrowhead pointed directly at my navel.

11

Death in the Hills

"You're early," he said. "I was delayed. I've only just gotten here. Have you made up your mind?"

I was standing against the light. It was dark in the little cabin, or comparatively dark after the sunlight outside. I saw what had happened. He had taken me for someone else.

There wasn't much in the cabin: a stove, which he had already gotten going in one corner by the chimney; a rough bedstead in another corner; a couple of hard chairs on one of which he was sitting; the diving gear spread out near the bed; the deal table that carried the harpoon gun and on which there were also various provisions and a little pile of paperback books.

At first sight his face looked open and honest, and then you noticed that his eyes were too close together and his mouth was narrow and greedy. His youth and his physical fitness prevented these signs from being readily apparent now, but age, I thought, might write his character more clearly across his features.

He realized his mistake after a moment. "Who are you?" he demanded. "And what are you doing here? What do you want?"

I noticed his fingers tightening around the trigger. He was

84

certainly a bit jumpy, not that I blamed him. I'd have been the same if I'd found a stranger at this sort of secret rendezvous. It was enough to make me realize I'd have to talk pretty quickly if I didn't want that harpoon in my guts.

"My name is Richard Graham," I said. "I'm a friend of Simon Herald. I hear you're interested in his house."

"Who told you that?" He was nervous all right or perhaps frightened, I didn't know. There isn't a hell of a lot of difference. One is a nice way of saying another. Anyway, I felt the same. He looked as if he might go off half-cocked at any moment, and, if he did, so would the harpoon gun.

"I'll come to that in a minute. Look, can't you put that thing away? I'm only here for a friendly chat. It makes me nervous."

"That's what it's there for. We'll leave it for the present. What's your chat about?"

"I'm not sure, quite. But some people are after my friend's house. They want it or something in it badly enough to kill. I mean just that—not threats or bluffing or buying out, but plain killing like we used to do in the war. Whatever it is, they want to get it."

"Where do you think I come in?"

"I'm guessing. Maybe I'm guessing wrong. You're an expert on illuminated manuscripts. You're pretty good, too, at inscribing them yourself, or whatever the right word is, I understand. Edgar Shanks had you out here some time ago, I gather. I'm just piecing together scraps of information I've picked up here and there. How am I doing?"

"Go on."

"I think you stumbled on something Shanks was up to, something that was dynamite. You wrote it all down in Irish in your beautiful illuminated script so that no one but yourself could read it, and put it somewhere safe. The people who sold Simon his house were right-wing French aristocrats, or so I'm told. They were friendly with Shanks. It's not impossible, for instance, that you were staying there or came over for a day or something and that you dumped it in that lake." My eyes went

85

to the diving gear beside the bed. "That would be a fine secret place to keep it unless someone guessed what you'd done. Then they'd be pretty anxious to search the lake, wouldn't they? And if you'd put it away nice and carefully down there, they might want a considerable time to do it."

"I'm not saying for an instant that there's a word of truth in all this. But suppose there is. What do you want?"

"I'd just like to know if I've guessed right."

"You're asking a lot, aren't you?"

"Maybe. I think you're in this for money. Whatever you've got hold of, it's a pretty rich secret to sell. I have a feeling you don't yet realize just how tough a game you're playing. Don't say I didn't warn you, anyway. I think you're likely to get yourself killed."

"You're talking in melodramatics."

"I agree to an expert on illuminated manuscripts it might seem like that. But melodramatics have an awkward way of intruding into real life these days, especially when one tries monkeying around with other people's ugly secrets."

"Nobody, except one other person, suspects I'm anywhere near here, and he only knows the general area. He hasn't the least idea of the placement of this hut. When you knocked, I thought he'd come after me and blundered on the hut. He's not due till tomorrow. I've only told him to come to the Col. He thinks I'm sleeping rough. But I've been in Corsica before. I'll give you that. I used to spend days in these mountains alone. I love them."

"I think I see what you are getting at."

"You brought up the melodrama, you know. I could kill you now and bury you and no one would ever be the wiser. Or at least until I have finished what I came to do."

But while we'd been talking, I'd been taking stock. There was plenty of room for me to move in. I thought I could take him long before his spear could get me.

"Not with that silly gun of yours, you couldn't," I said. "You may not know it, but I could knock you and it sideways without giving you a chance of getting into action. The man behind the

86

gun has his problems, too. That's what we were always taught, O'Beirne, and it's as well to remember it."

He laughed and leaned back in his chair. Then he picked up a packet of Gauloises from the table and threw them to me. I took one and threw them back.

"Don't do that either," I said, "to a stranger. It's an invitation to him to move in and take you."

"I see. Where did you learn all this?"

"We'll leave that out, too, for the moment."

"Wherever it was, perhaps I could use your help. You seem to know more about violence than I do. But I must have time to think. That's why I came here."

"You're stuck for money, aren't you? What have you been doing, putting your hand in the till, betting, women?"

"I've never had any money. I've fought my way up. I've seen everyone else living as they liked while I starved, yes, damn nearly starved, Graham, on the pittance I could earn writing and broadcasting. I started to bet to try to get some capital, thinking that with my brains I could beat the bookie. I got in pretty deep. Then I came out here to do a job for these people and stayed with them. I wanted to live as they do. I saw my chance and I took it."

"Take care you live at all. Who are you meeting?"

"I'm not going to tell you that, not yet anyway. Come back at midday tomorrow, alone. I'll have seen . . ." He checked himself. "I'll have made up my mind then. No one else can find me here. You weren't followed?"

"No."

He glanced at the gun and pushed it impatiently aside. "You may be right," he said, looking at it. "I don't know how to kill. Come alone remember. I can watch that road from higher up here."

I turned and went across the clearing. I still didn't trust him and didn't care for those eyes. I half-wondered if he'd change his mind and take a long shot at me with the harpoon gun. My shoulder blades itched a bit as I walked, but I made the trees all right.

It took me a couple of hours to get back to Simon's place. I timed it fairly carefully, as I thought I'd come early for my appointment tomorrow.

Simon was in his study listening to the news from Radio Monte Carlo. The others were on the beach, he said. Roddy, apparently, had been cooling himself off in the sea all afternoon. It was, Simon considered, the best place for him.

"You're sticking your neck out a bit, going back, aren't you?" he said when I had finished telling him what had happened. "Hadn't I better come along and sit on a peak and give covering fire?"

"I don't think so. He's sharp enough. He'll know all right if there is someone with me."

"I could use the other road, the one from Ghisoni, and work through the forest."

"You'd never come on the hut except by the track. It's hard enough to find that. I'll show you on the map, as best I can, where it is, and I suppose if I'm not back, say six o'clock, you'd better come a lookin' and a shootin.' "

"I don't like this much, Richard. In the first place it's I who ought to be doing this, not you."

"Perhaps, but we've got to play it the way the ball bounces, haven't we? And the ball happens to have bounced into my court."

"Well, all right. You always were a secretive sort of swine. But I don't like it."

Before I went to bed that night I opened a case I usually kept locked and lifted a couple of shirts which hadn't been unpacked and which still lay on the bottom. Underneath them was a Luger pistol, a very old and valued friend. I took it up, slid in the magazine, checked the action, and dropped it into a jacket pocket. Then I undressed and turned in.

I had disturbed dreams. I kept seeing the faces of O'Beirne and McKee changing and shifting and leering at me. Then I was riding a race; O'Beirne was the owner and the finish was somewhere on the quays at Ajaccio. I was winning by half a length and the horse I was beating was being ridden by a tousle-headed boy. No, by Jove, he was going to get up and beat me. His head and shoulders came up level with mine. I could have sworn I'd seen him before. I threw my whip away and turned around to get a better look. I had time to reflect that Roddy would have something to say to me on the subject of riding a finish. Then I woke up. That blasted tousle-headed boy, I thought. Then I grinned to myself. I didn't quite know why.

Immediately after breakfast I put the Luger in the glove compartment of the Renault and set out for the hills. Even though I knew the track was there, it was hard to find the exact place. There seemed to be no great need for concealment since he knew I was coming. So, once I had found it, I drove along it quite openly. There was a good deal of bouncing and scratching and brushing from branches, which didn't do the paintwork any good and would no doubt bring down Simon's wrath upon me later on. The Simca was still where I had seen it the day before. I swung the Renault around and backed in beside the other car. Then I took the Luger out of the glove compartment, pulled back the action to put a round in the breech, saw that it was on safe, and pushed it into the belt of my trousers.

At the edge of the clearing I halted. There was no smoke going up from the chimney of the hut. That was the first thing I noticed. Standing back behind the bole of a tree I looked the whole place over carefully. Something told me to take care. The door of the hut was ajar. Not much, but enough to make me wonder. I could just see the dark strip of an opening between the edge of the door and the jamb. Then I really smelled trouble, bad trouble. I took out the Luger and snapped off the safety. Holding it down at my side I walked quickly across the clearing. Nothing happened. I still wasn't taking any chances. I put my back to the hut beside the door. Reaching out a foot I gently kicked it open. It creaked and swung in. There was no movement from inside. From where I was, the place seemed empty. There was nothing much I could do but chance it. I went in quickly and on my toes.

The hut had been ransacked. That was the first thing I noticed. O'Beirne's few possessions were strewn all over the floor. Soles had been ripped off shoes, cans burst open, books torn apart. Then I saw him.

He was on the bed in a corner, huddled in a heap. One hand was up clutching his left side over his ribs. Through the fingers a dark stain was spreading. He had been shot, and at close range, with a small caliber revolver. He wasn't quite dead. As I bent over him, his eyelids flickered.

"Graham," he said, with a gasp. "You were right. Violence, didn't realize . . ." Then he made a sudden convulsive effort to fight free of what was coming to him. His eyes widened and brightened. "You want the koodhuck," he panted, at least that's what it sounded like. "It's all in the koodhuck. It's there, Graham." The struggle was too much for him. There was a sudden rush of blood and froth to his mouth. His whole body seemed to fold up and his head fell forward and rolled to one side. He was dead.

I straightened him out as best I could and pulled the eyelids down over the staring eyes. I looked around me. I was pretty sure there was nothing of use left in the hut. Whoever had gone through his effects had done his job thoroughly. What was that word he had used? Koodhuck. It was Irish, I supposed, but what the hell did it mean? O'Beirne must have thought he was giving me a vital clue when he panted it out with his dying breath.

Inadvertently I'd moved away from him toward the door. There was a sound outside like the breaking of a branch when it's sharply trodden on. Something brushed my hair and thudded against the wall behind me. There was the faintest movement behind the screen of trees.

Instinctively I jerked out the Luger and fired twice. I must have been more rattled than I knew, for I fired from the hip and anyone who does that with a Luger is asking for trouble. The spent shells shot up and hit me in the eye. Another shot came through the door too damned close for my liking. I flung myself aside. Then I tried working up to the window, and a shot promptly took out the glass and showered it on

90

top of me. I didn't seem to have a hope. Whoever it was out there, if he really wanted me, he only had to wait. Except that he probably didn't have all the time in the world either.

Silence came. Five minutes went by. That was according to my watch. It felt like five hours. A straw hat of O'Beirne's was lying on the floor. I picked it up, brought it to head height, and waved it just inside the doorway. No one shot at it. Then I began to be really frightened. What if someone outside was planning it just this way? Maybe they wanted me left here, afraid to make a dash for it, alone with a dead body. I'd have some explaining to do if the gendarmes came along, wouldn't I? After all, I had tried something like this at Ballymere myself. It might have given certain people ideas.

But if that was the plan, whoever was putting it into action would have to get to the nearest telephone. Where was it? If I was guessing right and the person outside, from the glimpse I'd had, was who I thought it was, then the inn with the banner across the road was the place they would make for.

If I was going to do it at all, it had better be now. Just the same, it was a chance to take on a hunch. He might be sitting outside with a rifle or what-have-you lined up on thte door. Well, maybe. I had to get out of here and the door was the only way. I couldn't afford to lose many more minutes. I thought I heard, very faintly, the noise of a car starting. That decided me.

I looked at the body across the hut. His sad little dreams of a place in the sun and a taste of riches were all over now. I lifted the Luger in mock salute. "So long, chum," I said. "I hope I'm not joining you."

I went out of the door sideways in a flat crouch with the gun up. No one shot at me. The silence was as absolute as ever, except for birdsong somewhere. I pelted to the car.

I didn't give a thought to the body paint as I bounded the car down the track, and I used the whole road on the corners coming down from the Col. Other traffic would have to take its chances. It didn't matter. There wasn't any. The place was empty, deserted, lonely, and as lovely as ever. The tall pines brooding upward were its only inhabitants. But I wished Si-

91

mon was driving. He could give me a beating at this sort of work. Then, far below me, I saw going away from me a little white open car. There was only one occupant. That meant the odds were my hunch was right. If so, I had to hurry. I took a few more chances and frightened myself, if no one else.

Once around the turn at the bottom of the descent the road was wide and open. That would help whoever was in front as much as it would me. I pushed the car up to its limit.

A white Guilia Sprint Alfa was drawn up outside the steps of the inn. That figured. I had a good guess who owned it.

There was a sort of patio set with tables at the top of the steps. A tall, good-looking waiter with a napkin over his arm was standing at the entrance to the passage leading to the dining room.

"The telephone," I shouted to him.

"*Là bas,* M'sieu," he answered, pointing. "*Mais c'est occupé.*"

I thought it would be. The inner hall was dark. There was a staircase with wooden banisters leading upward. The telephone booth had a small, rectangular window. The light was on inside.

I jerked the door open. A small fair head with tousled curls was bent over the receiver. I reached in and slammed it back on the hook. She was wearing a boy's checked shirt and jeans and had a small, tidy figure. I took hold of the shoulder nearest me and swung her around.

"I thought so," I said. "It's nice to see you with your glasses off, Contessa."

12

The Contessa

I took out the Luger and drove it into her ribs. She went up hard, into a corner of the booth. She looked hurt and frightened. She probably was.

Taking her by the arm, I pulled her out of the booth, up against me. "I want a word with you," I said, "several words. And one peep out of you and you'll get your lovely looks spoiled." I linked her arm with mine and walked her out across the patio into the sun.

The waiter looked as if he thought something funny was going on, but he said nothing. I didn't give him time. She was still in shock or pretty near it and I intended to keep her there.

In the car I said to her, "I mean it, in case you think I don't. You do anything I don't like and I'll belt you across the head with the barrel of this Luger. This is the second time you've tried to kill me, to say nothing of O'Beirne." I switched the ignition on and knocked the car into gear.

At the head of the pass I pulled off the road and into the pines. "Get out," I said.

She opened the door and stood beside the car. I came around toward her. "We're going to take a walk," I told her.

93

The turf was springy beneath our feet. We took a path at the edge of the pines. The whole panorama of the pass fell away below us. After a few minutes we came to a secluded place, a little oasis of grass in the circle of rocks. Far beneath us the black ribbon of road crawled toward the plains and the sea.

I leaned against the tallest of the rocks. It was hot up here, out of the breeze with the sun shining remorselessly down on us. The lichened surface of the rock was warm under my hand.

"How does it feel to kill in cold blood?" I asked her. "That's what you did, isn't it? With one of those little lady's guns that look like toys and aren't—provided you're near enough. Did you use your sex to get close to him? Was that how you managed it? I suppose you are a woman, Contessa, or are you?"

"I didn't kill him," she said.

"Oh, who did then?" I asked her. "He told me only one other person knew where he was. You were looking for him at the port yesterday. I suspect he wasn't as clever as he thought and that you'd known of his hideout since the last time he was in Corsica. You guessed right. He was blackmailing you, wasn't he?"

"Can't you stay out of this, Graham? You don't know what you're meddling in. You may be the next."

"I'll take damn good care I'm not. What was he blackmailing you with? What had he gotten that you wanted? You and Shanks and Manahan. You're all in a panic, aren't you? Frightened enough to kill. What is it?"

"Do you think I'm likely to swap him for you? Find out for yourself."

"I will. We're alone here and I'm bigger than you. I think you've got the gun that did the killing still on you. There's a bulge in your jeans over your luscious little bottom. Give it to me."

"Go to hell."

"The local gendarmerie will be interested in that gun, I

think. You know, you should have thrown it away. You can't get it out quick enough to use it on me. Hand it over."

She told me explicitly in four words of four letters what I could do with myself.

"Which was your finishing school?" I said. "I'll put it on my list. They seem to have taught you all sorts of interesting languages. All right. You asked for it. If you won't give it to me, I'll get it."

She tried to wrench her arm free. I pulled her toward me and grabbed at the zip of her back pocket. She struggled like mad. With her there writhing in my arms I felt a sexual excitement gusting up inside me and cursed myself for it. Ever since I'd first glimpsed her in the waiting room of Manahan's office it had been there, latent. Now it was a reality. You couldn't see her without wanting her. Some women are like that. It didn't do me any good with her now. It distracted my thoughts; and, what's more, she knew it.

She got herself out of my grip, sliding herself free with a laugh. The laugh brought me back to my business. I caught her as she turned to run. Her shirt ripped under my hands, but I grabbed her shoulder and held it. Together we both fell to the turf. She bit me savagely on the upper arm.

"Damn you," I said, slamming her back on the ground. The shirt flew open. There was only a vestigial bra underneath. She was a woman all right. The small breasts were round and proud, and as firm and hard as apples. But this time I was not to be distracted. My arm hurt like hell. She had teeth like a terrier's. I was going to get that gun. My fingers got to the zip and wrenched it across her soft buttock. Then I dug into the pocket. It was there, all right. I jerked it out. It was a beauty, a little pearl-handled Browning automatic, custom-built for the carriage trade.

She lay there, her eyes baiting me. They were very blue. Her cropped curls were blonde and pale against the green of the turf. Somewhere between us was the musk of sex and invitation. Stupidly, for the second time, I relaxed my grip.

She laughed and her arm went around my neck. She pulled me down on top of her. Her mouth opened under mine. Her tongue, sharp and soft and avid, was darting in and out of my mouth. My hand groped for the waistband of her jeans.

"God," I said pulling away, "did anyone ever tell you . . ."

She laughed again. "Yes," she said, "they all tell me when I want them to."

Then she kicked me in the crotch.

I had just sense enough to grab the gun as I rolled over in agony. While I writhed, she was gone.

As soon as I could stand, I walked to the edge of the drop. Far below me the Alfa was going like a streak of white down the road from the pass. Following her was useless.

I looked at the gun. It was a pretty little thing, all pearl and nickel, and it winked in the sun.

The safety was on. I put it off and tried the action. The magazine was full and there was a round in the breech. She'd had the time and the presence of mind to reload. If she'd thought of that, why hadn't she thought of throwing it away? Well, people do silly things under stress. That's how they get themselves caught.

Then, as it lay in my hand, something about it struck me. I lifted it to my nose and sniffed at the muzzle. There was no mark or smell of discharged cordite. I ejected the round and whipped out the magazine. The barrel was clean and unstained by powder. The gun had not been fired.

I stared at it in amazement. Then I put back the clip, set the safety, and dropped it into my pocket. Very thoughtfully I made my way back to the car.

"What on earth does koodhuck mean?" I asked, more or less at large as we sat with our brandies on the terrace after dinner.

"Damned if I know," Simon said. "It's Irish, I suppose, and none of us 'ere speak the language."

96

"And only a handful do in Ireland, I gather," Sue put in.

"That's where O'Beirne was so damn clever," I said. "The trouble was, poor devil, he was too clever by half. When it came to the point and he wanted to communicate, he couldn't."

"It wouldn't be the name of a horse?" Roddy suggested helpfully.

"Christ!" Simon said. "No, it wouldn't. What on earth have you got inside that skull of yours that passes for a brain?"

"He has a sort of automatic clock for calculating the speed of his own and other people's horses once the tapes go up," I said. "It's a useful substitute. I never had it. I used to wish I had. But we're getting away from the point."

"There must be someone," Sue said. "Would the British consul be any help?"

"He's a damn nice fellow, but he's hardly likely to know Irish or anyone who does. In fact, I don't see where, this side of London or Dublin, we're going to find out. Even in Dublin I don't know how you'd go about it," Simon said.

"You could ask Charles Coningsby Manahan for a start," I said. "I bet he'd have someone lined up pretty quick."

"For a small fee and a dinner at the Russell," put in Roddy, who was quite irrepressible. He helped himself to more brandy.

"I have to import that stuff from the mainland," Simon said, watching the level in the bottle sink.

"Do you? You are a chap for doing yourself well. I must say it's very good. Goes down like oiled silk." Roddy took a long swallow.

"And it's not meant to be gulped down like beer. Taste it, can't you?"

"Oh, I can taste it all right this way thanks. I say, Richard?" Roddy sat up with a jerk.

"Yes."

"What about that publishing pal of yours? You introduced me to him at your club once."

"Do you mean Robin Saunders? Well, what about him?"

97

"I think that was his name. Didn't you tell me he was a splendid old woman who knew all about everyone and everything in London?"

I doubted if Robin would be flattered at the description of himself, but I thought I saw what Roddy was getting at. "The clock seems to be working overtime and off the course tonight," I said. "But that's an idea. He might give us a line. Did you ever meet him?" I turned to Simon.

"No. I think I have heard you mention him."

"He's the chairman of Saunders & Renton. A dedicated publisher if ever there was one. One of his boasts is that he can lay his hands on an outside reader to test the authenticity of a manuscript on any subject in half an hour's notice. We could try him with this one. He might well have a line on an Irish translator. It can't do any harm."

"I suppose not." Simon didn't seem too pleased that it was Roddy who had come up with the suggestion. "You don't intend to tell the gendarmes about that poor devil up there in the hut, do you?"

"Not yet. I can't. They might pull me in. I want a couple of days anyway."

"You say her gun wasn't fired. If she didn't kill him, who did and why?"

"I don't know yet," I said slowly. "But I'd very much like to get inside that house of Shanks'. Part of the answer is in the lake, I think. The rest of it is there. I'm pretty sure of that."

Just then the telephone shrilled. It cut across the stillness of the night. We all looked at each other rather startled and surprised by the sudden sound. Mario appeared, soft-footed, at one of the doors to the terrace. The call, he said, was for Simon.

Putting down his glass, Simon muttered something and went off. He was back in a minute or two. "You're going to get your wish," he said abruptly looking at me.

"What?"

"Mr. Edgar Shanks desires our company for drinks tomorrow evening. He is so sorry he has been unable to ask us before, but he has had, don't you know, dear boy, pressing business commitments. He also apologizes for the short notice."

"Here's to a jolly evening," Roddy said. "I say, do you think the Contessa will be there?"

He and I reached simultaneously for the brandy bottle.

13

The Man Upstairs

As I shaved next morning I noticed a thin line of black coming up under my right eye. It would be bigger before evening. It made me remember the events of yesterday in vivid detail. I wasn't particularly proud of my part in any of them.

Downstairs I put a call through to Saunders & Renton in London. Mr. Saunders, they said, was available, and they connected me at once.

"Who?" he said in the abrupt way he has on the telephone. "Oh, it's you, Richard. Where are you?"

"I'm in Corsica."

"Corsica? I must say the line is very good. You sound as if you were in the next room. What's the weather like?"

"Marvelous. All sun and blue sky and warm sea and sand. And sin, I suppose, too, if it interests you."

"It's raining here and as cold as October. You do get around, don't you? What's that you said about sin? You haven't gotten yourself mixed up in something again?"

"Never mind. This conversation is costing my host a fortune a minute and I'd better get on with it. Robin, do you know what a Koodhuck is?"

"No, I don't. Should I?"

"I wouldn't really imagine so. The point is, can you find out?"

"I suppose I can, given time and a few more details. But, look, Richard, I've rather a day in front of me."

"Yes, but this is urgent. Isn't there a research bureau or something which you can call up?"

"How urgent? Really, Richard, you are always popping up at awkward times and asking difficult questions."

"Listen, Robin," I said, with what I hoped was low cunning, "there might be a book in this somewhere for you."

"A book? That does make things a bit different, I suppose. All right then. I'll do my best."

"It's Irish. That's the first thing."

"Yes, just to make it easier."

"It has something to do with illuminated manuscripts—or I think it has."

"Is that all you know?"

"Just about. The only reason I'm calling you, Robin," I said with more low cunning, "is that you're the one man in London who can help me in time."

He grunted. Then, like a hound owning to the first faint whispers of scent, he said grudgingly, "I do know a chap at the Victoria and Albert Museum, Arundell Browne, who might help."

"Call me back, will you?" I gave him the number. "I'll be here all day." I put the receiver down before he had time to argue, and went out of the house to the beach.

About four o'clock the call came through. I had been snorkeling aimlessly in and out of the rocks. When they called me I came in, picked up a towel, and walked to the house.

"Richard, is that you?"

"Yes, straight out of the sea, and I'm dripping water all over Simon Herald's Persian rug. Did you get a line on the thing?"

"Oh, yes, of course." He sounded smug. "It was surprisingly simple really. The chap at the museum knew immediately. There are not many of them around, it seems, and they are

101

much sought-after relics. Intrinsically useless, of course, and the stones with which they are embellished aren't even semi-precious. As an article on the market they're worth about six-pence. Thus they tend to be overlooked except by experts, who regard them very much as collectors' pieces."

"If you'd tell me what the hell they are, it'd be a damn sight easier to understand what you're talking about."

"Oh, yes. Just let me look at my notes." He coughed. "Well, a cumhdach—and that's how they're spelled, by the way c-u-m-h-d-a-c-h—is a portable case or book shrine measuring about eighteen inches by six inches. The literal translation is a cover. They were used by the ancient Irish to enclose old and valuable copies of the Gospels. They derive, if it's any use to you, from Egyptian book satchels. Sometimes the tribes took them into battle—as a sort of talisman, I suppose. Most of those in existence now have the books missing or have had them removed. This, of course, considerably reduces their value."

"Were the books always gospels?"

"The museum fellow wasn't quite sure about that, but he seemed to think so."

"Thanks a lot, Robin. You've done wonders."

I went back to join the others on the beach. Lying on the sand, I told them what Saunders had said.

"It's pretty obvious now," I said, "what happened. Shanks got hold of a cumhdach somewhere in Ireland, probably when he took over Ballymere Stud. Perhaps O'Beirne was staying there and recognized it and put him onto it. O'Beirne used to race a bit—he told me he was doing badly with the bookies. He probably was at Ballymere for after-race drinks or something and spotted it. Shanks is as vain as all get out. We know that from what we've seen and from the business of having his colors on his cars and wanting them carried again, in variation, on Ready Token. The cumhdach took his fancy and he got the idea he'd like to have the thing filled for impressing his guests. So he invited O'Beirne out here to write him an illuminated manuscript to fill it. Unfortunately for him, O'Beirne stumbled on or made it his business to find out just what Shanks is really up to in that place of his."

"That's all very well," Simon said, "but where do we come into the picture?"

"Well, this is what I told O'Beirne I'd guessed about him, and now I know I'm right. O'Beirne said it was all in the cumhdach. I'll guarantee he wrote down all he knew in Irish on the manuscript, letting on it was the Gospel. Since no one around here could read Irish, he was pretty safe. The people who had this place before you, Simon, were friends of Shanks. I imagine O'Beirne came over for a weekend or something, taking the cumhdach with him, making the excuse that he was going on working on it. Then he dumped it in the lake and high-tailed it for dear old Ireland on the first plane he could catch. That's my reading of it, anyway."

"And after a bit he started to blackmail them, I suppose," Simon said.

"Yes. The owners of this place moved out and you moved in. O'Beirne must have learned, somehow, that Shanks and Company were getting warm about where his secret was hidden. It was his private gold strike after all. He had to have it or he had nothing, and I suppose he was living it up by that time. He took the chance of coming out here and must have gotten a tremendous shock when he found this house had changed hands."

"Why didn't we find it, or Guiseppe for that matter when he went down?" Sue asked.

"You didn't, because you weren't looking for it. It's a pretty small object, after all. But my guess is that Guiseppe did find something. He saw enough to make Shanks certain the thing was there. Then he was interrupted or O'Beirne had hidden it so well, Guiseppe hadn't time to finish the job. But it's there all right, and Shanks knows it, and Guiseppe knew it. That's why they had to kill him, too, when they knew we were after him."

"Then, for all our sakes," Simon said, "I think we'd better get that damn thing out of the lake."

103

"So do I. The question is how to do it. I haven't the guts or the ability to go down into that dark hole."

"No more have I, and it seems no one else will."

Roddy coughed. "Er," he said, very hesitantly for him, "I don't mind having a go."

"Don't be an ass," Simon said. "What do you know about it?"

"I did a bit last year when I was with the Markhams in Greece. It's rather fun. Have you any gear?"

"Well, you're expendable anyway," Simon said. "Yes, there's gear here that came with the house. If it's not right we can replace it in Ajaccio."

"It'll have to wait until tomorrow though," I said. "We've an appointment this evening, remember?"

"Yes, by Jove, so we have. And it's over an hour's drive. We'd better be getting ready."

"You're not coming, Simon," I said.

"What?"

"We don't know what is behind this invitation. It may be to draw us all away. At any rate, Sue is better out of it. You'll both have to stay and guard the gate. Roddy and I will go."

Simon looked thunderous at this, and Roddy laughed. "You may cut it on his tombstone; you may carve it on his card," he chanted, "but a good man married is a good man marred."

"Great God," Simon said, "when did you pick up a taste for verse?"

"You suggested I should get educated some time ago, if you recall. I didn't, anyway. But I heard Richard quote that in the weighing room about a chap who was chucking it, and it stuck in my mind."

Simon showed us the way on the map. Then he folded it and handed it to us. He didn't at all care about the idea of being left behind. I saw him looking thoughtfully at the Mannlicher in the gun rack as I went upstairs to change. I felt rather sorry for Shanks' hired assassins if they started anything.

In the bedroom I found the Contessa's little Browning and dropped it into my pocket. It was less conspicuous than a Luger, and it could come in handy. Besides, she might like to have it back. I also noticed, as I brushed my hair, that my black eye was doing very nicely.

"Where'd you get that shiner?" were Roddy's first words to me as we drove away. "I've seen Sue looking at it all day and bursting her sides laughing. She thinks it's a present from the Contessa."

"The Contessa hits strictly below the belt," I said. "If you want to know, it's the result of being rattled and bloody stupid with a gun. Never fire a Luger from the hip, my boy. Let this eye be a lesson to you."

"If I fired a Luger from anywhere I'd more than likely shoot myself."

"Stay that way," I said. "You can know too much about guns when you grow up with them. And get to like them too much, too."

"Perhaps. I say, this country is pretty bloody beautiful, isn't it?"

"Simon says it's the last and the best place left in Europe. I'm beginning to think he's right."

"What are you going to do when we get there?"

"I don't know quite. I'll have to play it strictly off the cuff. If you see me passing out or doing something like it, don't take fright. I'll only be trying to get taken upstairs. I want to explore the house if I can."

"Maybe the Contessa will take you to her boudoir."

"That'd be interesting. It's probably hung with human scalps."

Maps of Corsica are neither numerous nor detailed, and with the development that is going on the roads keep changing all the time. Even with Simon's directions we had some trouble finding our way. Eventually, after bumping from pothole to ridge and back to pothole again over an execrable, dusty road, we came to a full stop facing a creek about a hundred yards wide.

The road ran on to a broad concrete landing stage. Moored in the creek were a couple of cabin cruisers, a racy looking

Chris Craft and a fifteen-foot yacht. A smart launch was alongside the landing stage. A man was standing by it, waiting for us. He was wearing a yachting cap, a white jacket and blue trousers. He turned as we came up. It was the man who had held me up at Malloran Park.

"Is it Mr. Graham?" he said blandly. "I have been sent to take you across."

"Don't be so damn formal," I said. "We've met before. This is the chap who hijacked me, Roddy. Care to push him in?"

"Yes, if you like," Roddy said cheerfully. "Hope he can swim."

The man's eyes went wary. He took a step sideways along the concrete and his hand hovered vaguely around his hip. "Really," he said, "there must be some mistake. I do assure you, Mr. Graham, I've never seen you before in my life."

"All right," I said, "we'll leave it for some other time."

"But I thought there were to be four?"

"Just two," I said. "Now hop in and get her started."

On the far side of the creek a short flight of steps brought us to a curving path. This was flagged and led through a clump of umbrella pines. Beyond them we came to the house.

It was a sort of Moorish palace built slap on the edge of the cliff. It was blindingly white with a red-tiled roof. There were towers and domes and minarets and whatnots, and it seemed to stretch for about half a mile. Sue hadn't been far wrong when she said it was getting along toward the Taj Mahal.

At a brass-and-iron studded door that wouldn't have disgraced the Alcazar, the man handed us over to a white-coated houseboy. Some sort of exchange took place between them, and I thought I saw our escort making a signal with his fingers to indicate there were only two of us. Then the houseboy led us along a vast hall floored in polished hardwood and down a big bright passage toward the seaward side of the house. He stopped outside a door from behind which came the muffled hum of several people talking together at the same time. There were other guests besides ourselves, it seemed.

On a long mahogany table near the door was, I noticed with a quickening of interest, a Colonel's kepi with a Foreign Legion flash and bars on it.

"Romantic looking headgear," I said to Roddy. "They never gave us anything like that."

"Didn't they? I thought you had a colored beret or something."

"Not me, chum. I was lucky if I got a cloth cap."

Inside the room, Shanks, immaculate in a blue lightweight suit, was holding court. Beside him was the Contessa in a slim white dress devoid of ornament except for a gold-and-diamond scarab on one shoulder. The dress looked as if it had come straight from Balenciaga; she looked an unsullied seventeen. As my eyes took her in, a tingle of static electricity stabbed through me.

"But where are my other friends?" Shanks asked as he fussed over to us, his hand held high. "The dear Susan Herald. Not ill I hope."

"A touch of la grippe," I told him gravely. "And Simon felt he couldn't leave her. He sends both their apologies."

"The Contessa you know, of course."

"Yes indeed. We've met in all sorts of interesting places. You might almost say we're intimately acquainted."

"Mr. Graham has hidden depths, Edgar," she said demurely.

"You must tell me about them some time, my dear." He gave a little teehee of laughter. He was enjoying himself. "And these are our other guests," he said.

They were the Foreign Legion Colonel from Bonifacio and his wife. The Colonel was in uniform and it was to him that the kepi obviously belonged. He looked hard-bitten, tough, and fit, and had the ease and fluidity of movement of the fighting man who has kept himself in training. A man to be wary of should he be against you, or even perhaps if he was for you, I thought, as I saw his peculiar, tawny, hooded eyes. I wouldn't have cared to tangle with him without a gun in my hand, or even with one, come to that. His wife was skinny and desiccated as if all the juice had been sucked out of her by the desert sun.

She presented no challenge to the Contessa. The guests were both drinking whiskey. His name was Gregorov—the same man who had been inquiring for O'Beirne on the quay. Well now, I thought, things are getting interesting.

As well as whiskey, trays of champagne and champagne cocktails were being circulated, carried around by white-coated servants. Roddy readily addressed himself to these and to the Contessa. As I sipped my drink, I saw Gregorov and Shanks in conversation. Gregorov said something, looked at me, and then looked quickly away as I intercepted the glance.

Three long casement windows opened onto a terrace. With the words, "Come and admire the view, dear boy," Shanks took me by the arm and led me toward one of these. He reeked of scent, or perhaps it was only eau-de-cologne for men of distinction. It's hard to tell nowadays. Gregorov followed us a pace or two behind.

Out in the sunlight where I could see him properly I thought Shanks looked old and ill. His eyes did not seem to be focusing correctly; his color was bad, and there was the sheen of sweat on his face.

"And what do you think of Ready Token, the dear Contessa's horse, Mr. Graham?" he asked me as we stood on the balcony. "Will he make a Gold Cup horse one day?"

I reflected that the horses that were likely to make a Gold Cup horse one day were just about as numerous as those who would have won the National if they hadn't fallen. I was thinking out a tactful answer when I heard near at hand a faint but distinct click, followed almost immediately by another.

The balcony on which we stood faced directly out to sea. In fact it seemed to hang over the edge of the cliff. Below and to the right was a little artificial harbor with what looked like a fishing boat in it. Crates were being unloaded from this and manhandled toward the shore. Shanks pointed down at the work.

"Sometimes we disembark our catch here," he said. "It makes transportation to parts of the island easier."

I turned to follow his arm and there was another click. I

wondered why I was being maneuvered before an unseen camera and why the hell they were photographing me anyway. I didn't like it much.

"But about Ready Token?" Shanks went on.

"Well, he won that race very gallantly," I said. "And he looks the part. But don't expect too much. He has a long way to go yet."

"Of course. I never expect too much, Mr. Graham. I'll tell the Contessa. I know she'll value your opinion." He gave a satisfied little teehee of laughter again, and hugged himself with the characteristic gesture of his kind. I felt rather like picking him up and dropping him into the sea.

At that moment from above our heads came the scrape of a chair being pushed back on a hard surface, followed by a long dry, hacking cough. I glanced upward. A balcony similar to that on which we were standing, belonging no doubt to an upstairs suite, was about four feet above us. I wondered who was in the house and not at the party.

Gregorov was at my elbow offering me a drink. In a deep voice which had all the implications of power and command in it and which was now pitched slightly above a conversational tone, he began to tell me how, on an exceptional day, one could see from here the Legion caserne in Bonifacio. Again from above came the cough—wracking, enduring, wretched. Gregorov frowned, his heavy brows coming together and giving his face an almost frightening expression of hardness and ruthlessness. He muttered something about there being a chill off the sea at this time of the evening. Then he turned back toward the room, almost pulling me with him.

"The air in Corsica can be very unhealthy, Mr. Graham," he said, looking me full in the face as he drew the casement windows closed behind him.

14

Queensberry Rules

A newcomer, I noticed, had joined the gathering. There was
no mistaking that tall, elegant figure. It was Charles Coningsby
Manahan. He appeared to be dispensing charm and patronage
all around the place. The Foreign Legion wife, who was waving a whiskey glass like a battle flag and who was teetering
pretty dangerously near the point of no return on her stiletto
heels, claimed Gregorov's attention. As a matter of fact, I think
he stopped to address a few well-chosen words to her. I crossed
the room to Manahan.

"Hullo," I said. "I thought you were safe in dear
old Oireland."

He was wearing a pearl-white tropical suit and the dark blue
tie of some Irish yacht club with harps and things on it.
He looked cool, capable of carrying off any situation, and
worth a million dollars. He probably was. Unruffled as ever,
he smiled at me. "Some urgent business turned up," he said,
helping himself to a glass of champagne. "Krug fifty-five, I
think. I prefer to drink champagne *au naturel* and not to
ruin it with brandy and bitters. Don't you?"

"No," I said.

"You disappoint me. I thought from our last conversation

that I had finally found someone civilized among the racing set."

"Do you think you could show me the bathroom?" I said. "I've had a hell of a long drive and . . ."

He laughed. "Really, my dear Graham, don't take me for too much of a simpleton. You can't seriously expect me to fall for that very juvenile suggestion. I've no doubt at all your object is to explore the house, or should I say 'case the joint,' which might, I imagine, entail knocking me on the head, an indignity to which I assure you I have no intention of submitting." He laughed again and took a sip of his drink. "It is Krug fifty-five, my favorite year. No, I have a rather better idea."

"Oh, what?"

He took out a fat gold case, the gift of a grateful client no doubt, and offered me a cigarette. As I bent to the spurting flame of his gas lighter, also mounted in gold, he said, "I do, however, want to see you and talk to you, Graham, but not here. I have a serious business proposition to put to you."

"Another?"

"Yes. I think you have some information which might be of use to me. Perhaps we can manage an exchange."

"Perhaps. Where do you suggest we meet?"

"When you leave here go to Propriano. At the end of the town, on the way to La Reina Banca, there is a café called Jake's Bar. Go there and wait for me. My dear Graham, how would you frame a handicap if say, Golden Miller, Mill House, Arkle, and Prince Regent were all in it?"

"What a fascinating topic. I wondered why you both seemed so engrossed. Would you include Cottage Rake?" Shanks was standing at our elbows. I had forgotten his catlike method of approach.

The Contessa was a few paces behind him. She was looking over his shoulder at Manahan. She appeared to be trying to convey something to him. There was an expression on both their faces I couldn't define at all.

Something in the way Shanks was speaking made me look

111

at him again. Once more I was struck by the peculiarly muddy color of his face. He also appeared to be having difficulty with his enunciation and in controlling his lower jaw. Probably he'd had too much to drink, yet it didn't look very much like drunkenness to me. However, alcohol takes all kinds of people in all kinds of ways.

"I wouldn't have him," I said. "He was a herring-gutted sort of horse. He never could give weight away. But here is Roddy. Why don't you ask him?"

"I know which of them I'd like to ride," Roddy said, helping himself to champagne. "Can't say I'm an expert at handicaps. Too many figures for me. Anyway, what did Golden Miller do? He was way back in the dark ages when they raced hunters, wasn't he?"

Shanks gave his little giggle. "That's the next thing to sac-sac-sacril . . ." His voice went off into a mumble. Then he said vaguely, "You know what I mean."

Both the Contessa and Manahan were now undisguisedly and anxiously staring at him.

"He beat the best they could send against him, giving them weight," I said. "None of the others have done that yet or are likely to. Or have won a Gold Cup and the National in one year. And you wouldn't call Thomond a hunter—or would you?"

"Next year no doubt Ready Token will come along and beat them all," Manahan said smoothly. But he was still looking at Shanks.

"I hope you'll let me ride him for you," Roddy said, seeming not to notice their anxiety.

"Ah, yes, you must ride Golden Miller, dearest boy," Shanks said again in that vague, imperfect speech. He moved off, stumbled a little, and recovered himself. Some of the champagne in his glass slopped over onto the floor.

Just then the Foreign Legion party made a move to go, and we followed them. I saw Gregorov studying Shanks intently as he took his leave.

"Well," Roddy said when we were in the car, "you didn't do

much exploring, did you? So far as I could see you spent most of your time gassing to that four-flusher, Manahan, about Cottage Rake."

"I did more than you think. He wants to meet me tonight."

"Who, Manahan?"

"Yes."

"Where?"

"In a place called Jake's Bar in Propriano. Did you notice Shanks?"

"Yes, I'd have a bit of a job to ride Golden Miller, wouldn't I? The old boy was as tight as a drum."

"I wonder."

It was dark when we reached Propriano. Down by the port "Jake's Bar" was spelled out over a doorway in neon letters which flicked on and off. I parked the car across the street, told Roddy to wait for me, and went in.

The place was gotten up as an imitation cave. There were rough rocky walls hung with fishing and snorkeling gear, seaweed, and suchlike. A bar took up one side; facing it was a row of low, well-made oak tables with settles behind them. An archway at the back appeared to lead into an inner room. I walked over to this and found myself in another imitation cave higher and larger than the outer one. The ground space of this was entirely taken up by a dance floor. No one was on it at the moment. In one corner on a raised dais a three-piece orchestra was getting ready.

I returned to the other room and took the table nearest the door. The place was almost empty. It was early yet, I supposed. There was a legionnaire with his white kepi beside him drinking pastis by himself, a few people standing at the bar, and, a table away, a French couple who ordered Cap Corse. I told the waiter to bring me a brandy and Perrier and set myself to wait.

I suppose because I wasn't expecting her, I didn't for a moment notice her when she came in. All at once she was standing at my table, still in the same white dress, the jeweled scarab glittering a little in the lights.

113

I got up. "This I scarcely hoped for," I said. "Where is Manahan?"

"Something detained him at the Casa d'Oro. He sends his apologies and asked me to come instead. Do you mind?"

"Not much. Aren't you taking a bit of a chance coming here alone to meet me? Remember what happened the last time. I might want to play rough."

"I like taking chances."

"So it seems. What will you drink?"

"Whiskey."

I ordered it. Then I sipped my drink and looked at her. She seemed to have it every way. Dress her down in slacks and a shirt or dress her up in something from the Paris collections and she looked a million in each. Some women get all the gifts. I didn't trust her an inch, but that didn't make any difference to the way I felt sitting opposite her and watching her.

When the drink came, she spun the glass around in her fingers. "Who killed O'Beirne?" she said. "I must know. You've got to tell me."

"Or tell Manahan. That's what you really mean, isn't it? Anyway, I thought you could tell me."

"I didn't kill him."

"I'm beginning to think you might just be right about that. You see, I've had a long hard look at your little gun." I took it out of my pocket and pushed it across the table to her. "Take it," I said. "It's a pretty little thing, and at close range as lethal as its owner."

"Stop fooling. I've got to find out who it was." There was urgency in her voice. That was sincere at least. "You didn't. You were there after me. I saw you."

"At least you admit you were on the scene. That's something."

"Of course I was. The fool, he was in love with me. He wanted me to go away with him. He kept talking about how he loved the hills, that he had somewhere we could be alone together away from everybody. I had him followed on one of his walks. I guessed that was where he'd go when he wanted to

114

hide. He was a bit of a creep, O'Beirne. I should have known he'd get up to something slimy. He whined when he was trying to make love."

"He'd be scarcely in your league in bed, I imagine, but that was hardly why you wanted him killed."

"We didn't want him killed."

"Oh, who did then?"

"Who was firing at you? That's who killed him. I tried to get near enough to see him and then you, you bloody fool, you started to shoot at me."

"Your command of idiom is splendid, Contessa. Do remind me sometime to get the name of that finishing school. So then, when you couldn't find out who the real killer was, you thought you'd phone the gendarmerie and try to pin it on me. Remarkable. You didn't learn that at Heathfield."

"Who was it? You've got to tell me."

"What if I don't know?"

"You know all right."

"Well, perhaps I could guess. Now I'll ask questions. Who is upstairs at the Casa d'Oro? O'Beirne knew, didn't he? That's why he was blackmailing you. That's why you were looking for him, isn't it, when you found he was here?"

"What are you playing at, Graham?"

"I don't like people who try to kill me and my friends, who think the laws of God and man weren't made for them. I think you and the people you're shielding or being paid by or what have you belong to that crew."

"Charles wants to see you," she said. "Will you come back to the Casa d'Oro with me?"

"No."

"Why?"

"That place looks remarkably like a fortress to me. And I'm remembering the conversation we had about the complaint doctor the last time you entertained me. And, by the way, don't bother to try flourishing the boudoir Browning at me. I took the precaution of taking out the clip."

She looked at me mockingly. "I thought you might be afraid

115

of something else," she said. "Though you don't look as if you'd whine."

"Some other time and place perhaps, Contessa," I said.

The strains of the band from the next room came through the silence which had suddenly fallen between us.

"Perhaps you're not afraid to dance with me," she said mockingly. "Or are you like most Englishmen? They dance as if they were wearing football boots."

"Racing boots in my case. That's quite an idea. Let's find out, shall we?"

We went together through the archway.

She molded her body against mine and looked up at me provokingly. "You must have forgotten those racing boots, Graham," she said. Then she put her head against my chest. Her hair and her scent were in my nostrils. She sighed. "Come back with me to the Casa d'Oro, Graham," she said.

"No."

She sighed again. Lifting her head, she looked at me. "Don't hate me too much, Graham," she said. "What I have to do, I have to do. Someday perhaps you'll understand."

Suddenly I became conscious that there were very few people on the dance floor and that the big Foreign Legionnaire was almost beside us.

At that moment the lights went out.

15

The Cumhdach

The Contessa had gone from my arms. I ducked and spun sideways. Something whistled down in the darkness and missed
me. A hand grasped my arm. I flexed my muscles to hit. A voice
said in my ear, "Over here, Richard, over here." It was Roddy.

"What the hell are you up to?" I snarled at him.

"Quiet. Look out," he said.

Someone else had heard our voices. A lighter snapped on. I
had a brief glimpse of the Contessa's bodyguard. It was only
brief. Roddy's right hand seemed to move about six inches. It
went into the man's stomach with a plonk. There was a sick
sort of gasp as he folded up. Roddy hit him under the chin as
his head came forward. It was all very correct and in the best
traditions of the manly art, much more straightforward than
the methods I had been taught. The trouble was that I didn't
think our opponents were very well acquainted with the
Queensberry Rules.

"Any more for the Skylark?" Roddy inquired of the room at
large.

"Come on you young fool," I said, "unless you want a knife
in your guts."

They were lighting matches and snapping on lighters in

the outside bar. We only just got away with it. Someone came at me as I reached the door. I got the point of my shoulder under his chin and he didn't come any further.

"Let's get the hell out of here," I said as we reached the car. "What happened?"

"I saw the Contessa going in, and a little later that creep who ferried us across came along. It didn't look too healthy to me so I went in after him. He was having a pretty intimate and sinister conversation with the barman. After a bit both of them went into the inner room and people began to come out. I strolled across to the doorway. You were lusting over the Contessa and dead to anything from the navel up. Very edifying. Can't say I blame you."

"That's something anyway."

"It seemed to me they were setting up to clobber you. There was a fuse box beside me. I kicked in the cover, put in my hand, and pulled out the lot. Hence the darkness."

"You ruddy young ruffian—but thanks."

"One good turn deserves another, old boy. You saved me from Bosanquet's clutches."

"Are we being followed?"

"Not bloody likely. I pulled the rotor arm out of the Alfa before I went in."

I began to laugh. "You ought to be doing this job, not me," I said.

"What job?"

That had been a mistake. I was tired and emotionally mixed up, which are things a man in my position has no business to be. I was finding treading a tightrope between friends and employers and enemies pretty wearing. Moreover, I was disliking it about as much as I've disliked anything.

"Trying to find out where the ruddy thing is and getting them to haul off their dogs," I said feebly.

I had other things on my mind, too. If Roddy found the cumhdach tomorrow, and I was pretty sure he would, then I had to get it translated. The only man to do that, so far as I could see, was Robin's chum in the museum, Arundell Browne. And I had to keep Deforge informed of what was going on.

There was a gas station opposite the café where Simon and I had talked to the old girl a few days ago. I pulled into it, told them to fill up the tank and check the tires. Then I suggested a drink to Roddy. He was never one to refuse. We crossed the road to the café.

It was busier tonight. There were two British parties from the holiday camp and some French couples from the nearby hotel.

The old girl wasn't around so I told Roddy I'd go and look for her. She was behind the service bar and in a bit of a tizzy dealing with all the business which she said was unusual. When I asked about the telephone she pointed vaguely to the back of the house. I found it in a dark narrow passage, an old-fashioned model fixed to the wall. I cranked the handle and gave the number.

The weather and the preliminaries I got through as quickly as I could. I hadn't much time.

"I may be on the verge of breaking this thing," I said. "Am I clear for London? I'll probably want a seat and a ticket the day after tomorrow."

"London is more difficult, but I shall see. They told us to use you. I think they will help. But remember, Graham, it will be a return ticket. You are in our hands."

"I know that," I said irritably. "Why do you think I got into this thing?"

"Can you talk?"

"No. It would be dangerous. And I'm in a hell of a hurry. One thing. Do you know of a Foreign Legion Colonel called Gregorov?"

I heard his breath go out in a little hiss. "So," he said.

"Well?"

"Call me tomorrow, Graham." The line went dead.

I paid the old girl for the call, got a whiskey for Roddy and a brandy for myself, and took them out to him.

119

"You were the hell of a time," he said. "I thought I'd have to go and rescue you again. No Contessa this time?"

"No. No Contessa."

"How well do you know her, Richard?"

"Know her? Just about as well as you do, except I haven't ridden a winner for her."

"It was she who set up that nice little trap for you. She got out from under when the fun began, but it was she who set it up. You know that?"

"I know," I said savagely. "Now will you shut up?"

I must have sounded pretty fierce, because he did.

Next morning I found the study littered with diving equipment. Roddy was checking it over with much the same care as he would have given to his tack before going out to saddle a horse.

"We went into Ajaccio yesterday," Simon said, coming in just then, "and had the cylinders recharged. I suppose he knows what he's about." He glanced at Roddy, who was fitting on the harness and adjusting it to size. "I gather you had an exciting night."

"You might call it that, I suppose."

"I see." Simon took a cigarette and gave me a curious look. "Who or what the devil is this Contessa? She must be an addition to the household. I don't recall her from the last time we visited."

"No. But that was some time ago, wasn't it? And you remember he mentioned her that evening in Propriano."

"She must be quite something. Roddy keeps talking about her all the time."

"She's quite something all right," I said.

Simon wanted to get the servants out of the way before we sent Roddy down, so we lunched early.

"A glass of cherry brandy and a cracker for you, my boy," I said to him, and to my surprise he agreed.

"I don't know much about this job, but I've learned enough to know you can't fool around with it," he said. "Any idea, Simon, how deep this place is?"

"Not much. But from what I remember it shouldn't be more than about twenty feet anywhere."

"That'll give me greater endurance time. If it's as dark as it looks I'll want a flashlight. Have you got one?"

"Yes. I checked it in Ajaccio, too."

"You know what you're looking for, I suppose," I said.

"Rommel's treasure," he said with a grin. "And I'm damned if I'm going to tell you when I find it."

After we had finished the meal and the last of the servants had putt-putted off on their scooters, we began to get ready in earnest. I think we were all a bit keyed up. I know I was. This, after all, was it. If Roddy was any good, and he gave the impression of being surprisingly capable, then we were going to find out if our guesses had been right and if the lake held the key to all the mystery and fear and violence which were now surrounding us.

Simon went off to his study and returned with the Mannlicher in the crook of his arm.

"What's that for?" I said.

"I have a feeling that our friends may have come to the same conclusion as ourselves—that it would be a good idea to search the lake. They may want to horn in. I'm going to sit on that hillock where we saw the man watching us the other day. I'll take damn good care they don't."

"Well, in that case," I said. I went upstairs and strapped on the Luger.

"Covering fire from two old gentlemen skilled in the art," Roddy said cheerfully. "First time I've ever noticed either of you so anxious about my welfare, I must say. Let's get this show on the road then. Richard, will you take the aqualung? No, don't lift it by that, you ass. That's the breathing hose. Try the harness. Sue, have you got the fins?"

We all trooped out into the sun.

121

When we arrived at the pool we put the equipment carefully down under Roddy's direction. Simon left us and began to walk slowly toward the little hill.

Roddy was stripped to his swimming shorts. He stared at the dark surface of the pool for a moment. Then he picked up the weight belt and clipped it on. After that he lifted the aqualung and strapped it into place over his shoulders. He took his time over this, examining each clasp as he fastened it, making sure the apparatus was secure and wriggling his shoulders to see that it was comfortable. Then he kicked off his espadrilles and pushed his feet into the fins.

"I'm going to try to quarter the bottom," he said. "I'll come up and report at halfway." He looked much as he did at the start of a race, a little tighter around the mouth and eyes but wholly in command of the situation.

We turned toward Simon. He waved to us to proceed, and I put up my hand in acknowledgment.

"Now all we want is a mermaid," Roddy said. He adjusted his mask, shoved the snorkel tube through his belt, and lowered himself into the water. He gave a quick flip of the fins. The dark oily waters swirled for an instant and then spread in ever-increasing ripples. He was gone.

Both Sue and I strained our eyes, but the dark, opaque surface defied all our efforts to penetrate it.

"I hope he'll be all right," Sue said anxiously. "This is a horrid place. It always makes me shiver."

It was, indeed, very still and, despite the sun, for some strange reason the pool itself seemed to cast a chill all around it. I was glad it was Roddy and not I who was down in it.

"The only danger he's likely to get into *is* with a mermaid," I told her with an assurance I didn't entirely feel. "And I don't suppose there are many of those about. Is he very precious, Sue?"

"He's my brother."

"Would you have tried to get Simon to sell the place against his will if it would have gotten Roddy out of trouble?"

She thought for a moment, her arms clasped round her knees,

122

her chin resting on them. "No," she said. "No, I wouldn't, though I might have hated myself and Simon too, I suppose, for not doing it. But you know Simon, Richard. Once he has his teeth into a thing he'll never let go. And he is everything to me, everything. Funny, isn't it?"

"No," I said, "not at all funny. I only wish I'd met you before he did. But that wouldn't have gone either, would it? I'm one of those guys who goes for the wrong woman and then never gets her."

"Perhaps. Maybe you're looking for too many things or for something you'll never find. Is she very lovely?"

"Who?"

"Your Contessa, of course. Simon says you're mad for her, that's why you're being so secretive about everything. Golly. I shouldn't have said that, should I?"

"Simon says that, does he?" I got to my feet and threw a pebble into the far part of the lake. "Maybe he's right. Does he think she killed O'Beirne?"

"He doesn't know. None of us knows. How can we, Richard, when you only tell us bits and pieces. . . ."

"Does he think I killed him? Do you?"

"No, neither of us do. But the thing is, Richard, you've been mixed up in so much, I don't think you care an awful lot any more what happens to you. Especially the way you're feeling now after being crossed in love or whatever happened to you. Simon was like that when I first met him. It's latent in you both. It's a side of you both that terrifies me. It always has."

At that moment Roddy's head broke water. He swam toward us and pulled himself to the bank.

"Nothing," he said, pushing up his mask. "Absolutely nothing. It isn't as deep as all that and for some extraordinary reason it's quite easy to see down below. There's a sandy bottom with steep sides beginning about fifteen feet down. I've been over every inch of it. There's no Rommel's treasure, no box, and no mermaid. You can take that for sure."

"What about the other end?"

"Can't say yet. I only had a glance at it. It seems to widen out

123

a bit on the bottom there. I'll go and have a look. I think we're on a loser myself. How big did you say this thing was?"

"About a foot and a half by six inches."

He was down for longer this time. We idled in the sun, chatted, and kept glancing surreptitiously at our watches. Up on the hill Simon sat, his rifle across his knees, constantly turning to look at the country below him. A scented breeze licked across the maquis, ruffling the waters of the lake. The sun beat down. It was hot enough to overcome the chill coming off the lake, or most of it.

At length, with a splash, Roddy broke water and swam over to us. This time he seemed excited.

"I think I'm onto something," he said. "There's an underground stream plumb at the far end. Beside it is a clump of rocks and stones. Someone has been at work on them, moving them. An opening in the side of the thing has been uncovered. It looks as though you were right and whoever it was hadn't time to finish the job. Only part of the opening or door or whatever is unblocked. Not enough for anyone to get in. But I think I can make room to get through. If I do, I'll be in. In case I don't come back send down a diver. It might be the Loch Ness monster down there. You never know your luck."

"Or a harem of mermaids," I said, but he was gone.

We waited in a fever of impatience. Ten minutes passed and then twenty.

"How long do you think we ought to give him?" Sue asked.

"Damned if I know. I don't even know the endurance of those things. I wonder if he does."

"He said something about it not being deep giving him a longer time down. I hope . . ."

Then suddenly he was back. He swam strongly toward us, kicking out with the fins. There was a bundle in his arms.

"Got it," he said triumphantly as he climbed ashore.

It was a box-shaped object all right, of about the right dimensions. Sailcloth wrapping, carefully stitched and sealed, covered it. I picked it up. It was light, but I could tell there was something inside it, something which slid against its sides as I tilted it. Turning toward the hill, I gave a thumbs-up signal to Simon, beckoning him to come down.

Roddy was stripping himself of his gear.

"Where was it?" I asked.

"In a sort of underground gallery. I got the entrance open with a bit of work. They must have been damn near it when they were interrupted. That's what makes them so mad, I suppose. The opening was just big enough for me to get into with all this stuff on my back. There was a short passage going up and then this gallery with stone shelves on either side."

"Some sort of prehistoric tomb," I said. "Was there anything on the shelves?"

"Nothing except that box affair. I had quite a job to find it. At first I thought the whole place was empty. Then I figured I'd better do the job thoroughly when I was there. I went over each shelf and right at the end, pushed to the back of one of them, was that thing. I wasn't sorry to get out. Creepy sort of place. Christ I'm cold."

I looked at him. Gooseflesh had broken out all over his chest and arms and he was beginning to shiver.

"We'll take that stuff," I said. "Get back to the house as quickly as you can and have a hot bath and a large shot of Simon's best brandy. I guess you've earned it."

In a minute or two Simon joined us. I told him what had happened.

"See any one?" I asked.

"No, but it's not quite as good an observation post as I thought. There's a lot of dead ground on the seaward side and you could lose an army in that maquis. A sail boat has been hanging around most of the afternoon, but it's probably only someone from Isobella. They come by all the time."

We gave the box to Sue, picked up the gear, and walked to the house. Simon went to his study to put the rifle up and Sue, murmuring something about tea, disappeared toward the kitchen. I was left alone, staring at the box and itching to unwrap it.

They all came back at much the same time, Sue with a tea

tray, Simon with a clasp knife, and Roddy with a bottle of brandy and a glass.

"We'll give Sue the honors, I think," Simon said, handing her the knife.

We all bent forward as she slit the stitches. The sailcloth wrapping came away easily. Underneath was another covering of oiled silk. Beneath that again was a second one. O'Beirne had done his work of preservation carefully.

By this time we could see the outlines of the object. It was indeed a box with a dull sheen on it which came up through the silk. Sue cut the last coverings free and what we had been searching for lay exposed on the table.

It was a rectangular container made of some grayish colored metal with silver scrollwork on its face and stones set into the silver. Whether they were precious or semi-precious stones I hadn't the knowledge to tell. They gleamed in the light. The center one, I remember, was oval-shaped and a dark red color. The color of blood, I thought.

"Open it," Simon said.

Roughly-made catches were set into the right-hand side. Sue unclasped them and lifted the lid. Inside, again wrapped in oiled silk, was a manuscript. Sue took this out, laid it on the table, and gently pulled away the silk.

It consisted of parchment sheets bound up into a book, with stiff covers overbound in manilla paper. We crowded around Sue as she opened it and turned the pages. The ms itself was modern—that much was obvious even to our eyes. The lettering, much of it illuminated, was beautifully done. The workmanship of the whole thing was exquisite. But it was in Irish. It meant nothing to us.

"Well, that's it," Simon said, throwing himself back in his chair. "Now all we want is someone to translate Erse for us."

"There isn't a crib tucked away somewhere, I suppose," Roddy said, refilling his glass.

"I'm afraid the only crib was in O'Beirne's head," I said.

"Yes, that's why she killed him," came a voice from the terrace. "Now I'll trouble you to stand away from the table and hand over that box."

McKee was in the doorway, his huge frame almost filling it. In his hand was a long-barreled Colt automatic. It looked almost grotesque in his great paw. But it was held remarkably steady. It was, I noticed with interest, a Colt Huntsman of .22 caliber.

16

Old Man Remember

There was silence in the room. Sue, almost instinctively, had moved behind Simon's chair. Roddy was frozen with the glass halfway to his lips. I stared down the long barrel of the automatic.

"I suppose he came in off the sail boat," I said to Simon, and then, "you know, you're wrong about one thing, McKee."

"And what's that, Mr. Graham?"

"She didn't kill him."

"Who did then?"

"You did."

"Aren't you being a little far-fetched, Mr. Graham?" The half-servile, half-mocking manner was there still.

"I don't think so. And I'll tell you why."

"Yes, do that. It might be interesting—sir."

"You've been living on your wits too long, McKee," I said. "I think you were in a bad run of luck. You were very anxious to get my fifteen pounds the other day, remember. You knew O'Beirne was onto something; you thought it was something good and you guessed he needed help. He was nervous and out of his depth, and he played into your hands by making those inquiries about this house and about Shanks. You tried

128

to get him to cut you in then and there and he told you he wanted time to think. He arranged to meet you up in the mountains after he'd had that time. He told me only one other person knew he was there. I see now he must have been thinking of you. He didn't know that the Contessa had found out where his hut was. Once he was there he thought he was safe. You made the mistake of giving me his address in Ajaccio, but you wanted the money and you thought he'd have left it long ago. By an unfortunate chance for you, he was delayed and I was able to follow him. You met him the next day and either killed him in cold blood and ripped the place to pieces trying to find his secret or else had a row and did the same. Either way it doesn't matter. Then the Contessa came along and after that I did. You must have gotten quite a fright. So much so that you tried to kill me as well. I suppose you intended to leave me there and let the police puzzle it out."

"You're trying to pin this on me," he said mildly, "and it won't work, Mr. Graham. She was there and so were you. You both had guns."

"Yes," I said, "but there's this difference. Hers hadn't been fired and mine isn't the same caliber as the gun that killed him. It was a small caliber gun. Like the one that you've got in your hand, McKee."

He straightened up and his eyes narrowed. "And how are you going to prove that?" he asked.

"Ballistic tests are accepted evidence nowadays," I said. "They'll compare your gun with the slugs they take out of him. Then we'll know if I'm right, won't we?"

"I don't think you're going to be able to make that test, Mr. Graham," he said. "But first we'll have that paper and the box. Tell the lady to bring it over to me. And she'd better keep out of the line of fire, you know," the half-humorous note had come back into his voice again. "You gents shouldn't get mixed up in this sort of thing."

"That's right," Simon said from the end of the table. "Take the box to him, Sue, like the nice man says. And keep out of the way."

Sue came around between us, picked up the manuscript, put it in the box, and started back behind Simon toward Mc-Kee.

The tone of his voice told me that Simon was up to something. Out of the corner of my eye I could see him tilting backward in his chair.

Sue went very slowly and carefully around the edge of the room, the box held out before her.

Something in the air warned McKee. His eyes went wary. He was going to have a job watching us all, and he knew it.

Sue went on. No one else moved. The muzzle of McKee's gun moved in a small arc across the three of us. Sue was halfway across the room. I wondered if Simon might be leaving it a bit late. Then he gave a shout and kicked himself in a back somersault off his chair.

For a split second McKee hesitated, swinging his arm toward Simon. I had all the time in the world. I took out the Luger and shot him in the shoulder.

The impact spun him around and slammed him back against the door jamb. His gun went off all right, but not in the required direction. The bullet ploughed a sliver out of the table beside me. Then the gun clattered to the floor.

Sue screamed and dropped the cumhdach. Simon was off the floor and had his arms around her. The room was filled with the roar of battle and the stink of cordite.

"My, my, you old gentlemen do play it rough," Roddy said. The glass of brandy was still halfway to his lips. I noticed that none of it had spilled.

"Do something instead of sitting there like a television commentator," I told him. "Put a handkerchief around his gun and bring it here."

"Teamwork, McKee," Simon said, filling a glass of brandy for Sue. "One of the discredited virtues these days, but it comes in handy now and again. Can he hear me or have you killed him, by the way?" He looked at me.

"I don't imagine so." The Luger steel-jacketed .30 bullet is more remarkable for its penetration than its stopping power.

In all probability it had gone straight through. McKee had had an almighty slam on the shoulder and a nice clean wound. I didn't think he was badly hurt.

"Don't move, McKee," I said, "or I *will* kill you. It'd solve a lot of problems if I did."

Sue gave a little gasp and sat down.

"Just what are we going to do with him?" Simon said.

"Hand him over to the police, of course. There's a body up in the mountains that has to be explained away sooner or later. But I think we'd better bring the British consul into it now. What's his number?"

"It's in the telephone list in the study."

"All right. Here. Watch him, Simon." I slid the Luger along the table to him. In the study I kicked the door shut behind me. Then I put my finger on the catch of the telephone index. When I had found the number I cranked the lever on the telephone. It was the same old-fashioned call exchange that served the tavern down the road and I had to wait. This I did with very little patience. I was in a hurry, for I had another call to make.

The consul was in Bastia on business and would not be back until the next morning. No, they said, they didn't think they could get him; he was spending the night with friends on Cap Gorse.

I put the receiver back. I cranked it again and gave Deforge's number.

"The *libecchio* has gone," I said when the answer came.

"It is a blessing. One can only hope we don't get the *tramontane*. . . ."

"I must go to London tomorrow. I think I have what we want. Am I clean?"

"Perfectly."

"Can you get me a seat?"

"*D'accord.* Be at the airport at 9:30. There will be a message for you at the desk. As I have said, the ticket will be a return. I'm trusting you, Graham."

"You'd better, hadn't you?" I said grimly.

There was a pause. Then he said, "What have you found?"

"I'm not quite sure yet. That's why I have to go to London. I want to get some Erse translated."

"How long will it take, a day?"

"Yes, if I can get hold of the man I want." I hoped Arundell Browne was not on leave. But if he was, presumably the museum would know of someone else.

"Very well. Ring me from London, please." There was a click as he replaced the receiver.

A sound at the doorway made me look up. Simon was standing there. His eyes were as cold and unfriendly as flints.

"Just what the hell do you think you're playing at?" he said.

17

Gospel Truth

I sat in the Caravelle on the runway of the Ajaccio airport waiting for take-off. It was going to be a longish trip. They had to
route me through Marseilles. Although it was only a few minutes before eleven the sun glared down on the thin strips of
metal that surrounded us and, in common with most of my fellow travelers, I sweated and gasped. Many of them were vainly
twiddling the air-conditioning knobs. I knew better than that,
though why the Caravelle, which is one of the world's great
airplanes, doesn't let you have cool air on the ground where
you want it instead of waiting until you are at twenty thousand feet when you don't is something I have never been
able to understand. I also spared time to wonder why one sub-
jected oneself to being encapsuled in a tin tube, crammed
knee to chin along with others, roasted like a prawn in a pot, all
in the interests of speed and progress. Years back, people on
an errand like mine would have taken a boat and liked it. I
stared out at the heat shimmering on the cement, the coarse,
parched grass beside the runway, and the distant airport buildings, and wondered if it was all worth it.

In this instance it probably was. Things were approaching
some sort of climax, if only one knew what. No doubt the cumh-

dach translation would provide the answer. Which brought me back to things I had been trying, unsuccessfully, to push out of my mind.

Why did I always succeed in getting my personal relationships into an unholy mess? Professionals in this job should have no personal relations, no feelings, and no friends. It looked as though I was getting precious near that state.

I remembered all too clearly Simon standing in the doorway last night, staring at me as if I were something particularly obnoxious and slimy which had just crawled out from under a stone.

"So you're mixed up in it too, are you, Richard?" he had said.

"Look, Simon, I want to take that thing to London and get it translated."

"So I gathered. May I remind you it's mine? How much are they paying you? Or are you taking over where O'Beirne left off?"

"Dammit, Simon, I'm trying to help you."

"You're going about it in a strange way, aren't you? You come down here shot full of holes. I don't know what you've been up to and I don't want to. But as soon as you arrived, the moving in on this place got worse."

"Simon, you don't think . . ."

"I'm telling you what's been happening. You take over the running of my show and you play it, I'll remind you, pretty close to the chest. Whenever any of us try to find out what you are up to, you throw a stall. I know you always were a secretive bugger, Richard. I went along with you up till now. You'd better talk, Richard, and it'd better be good or I'm slinging you into the hoosegow with our friend outside."

I looked at him. I knew him too well not to realize that he meant what he said.

"What happened between you and the Contessa last night?" he went on.

"Nothing."

"Don't be a damn fool, Richard. Women have always made
134

a monkey out of you. A certain sort of woman anyway, and she's one of them, from all I hear. It may interest you to learn that I know one of the girls in the Air France office. I happened to ask her how you got that ticket to Dublin the other day so quickly at this time of year. You didn't get it; someone else got it for you. Either you're in with Shanks and Manahan —and I'd hate to think it . . ." He was cooling down a bit, I noted with relief. "Or else you're working for the types who have employed you before. I can't say I care much about them either, if you want to know."

"Neither do I, if it comes to that," I said.

"You've gotten yourself into a proper mess, haven't you, Richard?"

"You can say that again," I said.

He threw himself into a chair and reached for a cigarette. "All right, talk," he said.

There was no way out. I knew he was trustworthy. I talked.

"Undercover work is a dirty business if you do it properly," he said when I had finished. "There's no way around that one. And the dirt sticks. That's why, after the war, when they wanted to pull me into it, I dodged. You didn't. Do you know what's behind this panic? What Shanks and Company are up to?"

"No." I'd had a guess all right, but guesses weren't knowledge. "I think it's all in that manuscript. That's why I want it translated."

"If it's something fairly big, why is it getting such low priority at your end? You say there's only this chap in Ajaccio and yourself."

"As far as I know, yes. That's bothered me, too. It may be they don't want to step up things too soon, but I don't think so. I think the man in Ajaccio (I hadn't told Simon his name and he hadn't asked me) is ambitious. I think he's playing it down to his bosses. He wants to spring a coup and take all the credit himself. He doesn't strike me as being the brightest. There's probably a black mark against him somewhere. He wants to wipe it off and get a few plusses."

135

"Do you think the Legion is in it? That Colonel, Gregorov, seemed pretty thick with Shanks."

"I think they might be—or some of them. If they are, then it's big all right."

"Hmm. Well, I suppose I believe you, Richard. You can take the damn thing and get on with your job. But look, Richard . . ."

"Yes."

"I don't like your job. I'm not sure I care about you any more. Take your bags, will you? And don't come back until we ask you."

He went out, shutting the door carefully behind him.

I sat on, staring at the model of the blower Bentley on the mantelpiece, symbol of a lost, forgotten youth, and wondered where everything had gone wrong.

The roar of the jet engines beginning to run up broke into my thoughts. The aircraft pivoted and pointed down the runway. Again my thoughts reluctantly went back over the past twelve hours.

The next morning we met together in the study. Simon had arranged to bring McKee in to the British consul. He told me curtly that I could have the Renault and that they would pick it up at the airport later on. The atmosphere between us had been very strained.

I thought Simon was being unnecessarily hard-nosed, not that it surprised me very much. Once he got an idea into his head you couldn't shake him.

As I was starting the car, Sue came to the door. "What's up between you two?" she asked.

"Hasn't he told you? I'm an undesirable. I mix with the wrong people and my feet smell."

"Don't be a fool, Richard. He says things and regrets them, and he's too proud to admit it."

"Perhaps. Good-bye, Sue, and thanks."

"For heaven's sake, Richard. You're both behaving like prima donnas, as far as I can see. Richard, if you want his help I know he'll still give it."

136

"Thanks again. He hasn't said so, though. Tell Roddy I've been warned off, will you?"

"I'm not going to let you go like this. Simon'll start hating himself in a minute. If you want us, you've got to come to us. Promise?"

"All right, Sue. I always said you were my favorite woman. I promise." I kissed her then and drove out of the gateway.

I lunched at Marseilles airport, and then I was in another Caravelle climbing northward for London.

It was cold and raining in London, and the wind whipped at my thin suit. I left the airline bus, walked up the ramp, and took my place in the queue for the passport desk. I hoped Deforge had done his stuff. It was strange how, even after the few encounters I'd had with him, he had inspired no confidence whatsoever.

The customs officer began leafing casually through my passport. Then he saw the name and the photograph at the same time. He paused, looked again, put his finger in the passport to mark the place, and consulted a list beside him. Pulling a pad toward him, he made a note. He glanced quickly up at me and again at the photograph. Then he turned over the pages, banged the stamp down, and handed the passport back. He didn't look at me again. I went into the lounge to wait for the luggage to come up.

There was, as usual, a delay, so I crossed to the telephones and put a call through to the Victoria and Albert Museum. I asked for Mr. Browne. The operator said something about an extension. There was a racket going on as there always is, what with that low ceiling, the speakers squawking, passengers talking, and the people on the phones on either side shouting to make themselves heard.

Presently there was the click of a receiver being lifted and a voice said, "Browne. Ancient Manuscripts Department."

I shoved my finger into my free ear. That made things a little better, but not much. "Mr. Browne?" I said. "My name is Graham. I'm a friend of Robin Saunders. I think you know him."

137

"Oh, yes indeed. How is he?" The voice was high and pleasant.

"Very well, so far as I know. Hunting authors and manuscripts, just as usual. I don't know if you remember, but a few days ago he made an inquiry from you about a cumhdach."

"I do indeed. They're most uncommon things, you know."

"Well, that inquiry was for me. I've found one."

"Good heavens." He sounded excited. "How on earth did you do that? Have you got it with you?"

"No. But I've got what was inside it."

"A Gospel! I say!"

"I'm at London Airport and all bedlam is going on around me. Can you hear me?"

"Yes, but not very well."

"I'm not sure if this thing is genuine. Can I bring it around to show you?"

"By all means. I'd be uncommonly interested. But it's after four now and it will be some time before you clear customs, won't it? Would you mind coming to my flat?"

"No, of course not."

"Come along then, Mr. Graham. The address is 274 Eyre Mansions. It's just off Kensington High Street, but it's rather hard to find. If you're in a taxi tell him it's beside the firehouse. It looks rather like a warehouse from in front so don't be surprised."

"I'll be with you as soon as I can."

A few minutes later we were called to collect our luggage. My bag came up among the first. I took it across to the customs man who scrawled his hieroglyphic on it without a question. He must have been briefed. A porter lifted the bag to the moving track.

I went downstairs and got a taxi. I expected that the people here would keep an eye on me. I was a fairly bad boy after all. They'd know by now that I'd arrived. Whether I'd get any help if trouble came along was another matter. They might well confine themselves to an absence of hindrance. At one point in the journey I did look back and thought I saw a cab following us, but later on it appeared to have vanished. I put it out of my mind and thought about Browne.

I hadn't told him yet I wanted him to translate the thing. I supposed he'd do it, but I might have some difficulty with him if he found what I expected in the translation. I thought I'd have a good look at him before I committed myself.

Eyre Mansions was stuck in a dog-leg cul-de-sac at the end of which was the firehouse. Moreover, it did look more like a warehouse or a Victorian prison block than flats. Inside were broad low passages floored with wood parquet and paneled in faded fumed oak. The windows had stained-glass sides. A huge creaking elevator took me up.

The flat itself was a pleasant surprise. Even if the rooms had that indefinable lack of proportion stamped by Victorian builders on everything they did, they were bright and airy and large.

Browne's wife, a harassed-looking woman with wispy fair hair, led me out of a boxlike hall into a big drawing room. A couple of children, aged about four and five, were playing with toys on a worn carpet. There was a chintz-covered sofa, fat comfortable armchairs, a Chippendale tallboy which looked genuine, a claw-and-ball table with a tray of drinks, and books and magazines lying about everywhere.

"Dell!" she called.

A door opened in the far wall and a man came out. "Mr. Graham," he said, and I recognized the high, pleasant voice I had heard on the telephone. He was wearing loose tweeds, a white shirt and a tie made of rough, plain-colored material. He was, I suppose, about forty years of age and had a thin intelligent face. His hair, which he wore brushed back, was beginning to be streaked with baldness. "I expect you could do with a cup of tea after your journey," he said with a smile.

"Yes," I said, "if it's not an infernal nuisance, I'd love one."

"Marjorie, will you get us some tea? Milk or lemon, Mr. Graham?"

"Lemon, if that's all right."

"Of course. Do come in and let us see what you've got. It sounds most exciting."

I liked him on sight. The room beyond was a study. It was long and narrow and its walls, except for the space over the fireplace, were entirely taken up with bookshelves. Books were all around here too, spilling onto the floors and standing in piles on the huge desk in the middle of the room. On the desk, as well, was a stack of what looked like examination papers.

"A levels," he said, following my glance. "I'm one of those beasts of burden, an examiner."

"Hard work, isn't it?"

"It can be if you're conscientious about it. It's the borderline cases that worry you, you know. The tops and the bottoms are easy. Still, I'm lucky. I have a good board. It makes all the difference. And it brings in a little cash to supplement museum pay—and to buy books."

His wife came in with the tea tray, put it down, and left us.

"Now, Mr. Graham, let's see what you've got." He stretched out a hand. He was obviously itching to get at it.

I opened my bag and brought out O'Beirne's handiwork. He took it and looked at it, turning over the pages. He stared at some of the lettering for a little time, considering it. Then he closed the manuscript. I could see from his face that he was disappointed.

"This is beautiful work, Mr. Graham," he said at length. "But I have to be quite frank with you. It's modern. It's a fraud."

"That's not really such a disappointment," I said. "I had a pretty good idea it might be, but I wanted confirmation from an expert. Perhaps it's not quite fair to call it a fraud. It's more of a rich man's folly really. The writing is Erse, isn't it?"

"Well, er, yes. It's Irish, not Erse, don't you know. There's no such word as Erse. Sorry to be pedantic."

"Doesn't matter a bit. I'm not a scholar, as I'm sure you can see. Look, you can read it, can't you?"

"Yes, I can do that." He reached out and started to fill a pipe.

"I've an idea it may not be a Gospel at all, that whoever did it wrote down something else."

140

"I see." He looked down at the manuscript on his knees. "You know, from what I've already read, I don't think you are right. It's not quite finished, of course. There are one or two blank pages at the end, but you know that. I really don't think you can be right."

I couldn't believe it. I had been so sure all along that it was the key to the whole business, that O'Beirne had written down in it all he knew about the Casa d'Oro. If I was wrong, why had they been so anxious to get hold of it? Why had O'Beirne told me about it in his dying words. "It's all in the cumhdach," he had said.

"But," I said, "of course, I have no doubt you're right. I know it's an imposition, but it really is rather important. Could you go through it for me and tell me if there is any part of the text which is an interpolation? I'm almost certain there's a message in it somewhere that isn't Gospel at all. It may be a short passage or a long one, I just don't know."

He gave me a curious look. "I see," he said slowly. "You think whoever fabricated this buried in it somewhere a message or passage completely out of context?"

"Exactly."

"Just who or perhaps what are you, Mr. Graham?"

"I don't think I can answer that."

He looked at me for a long moment, drumming his fingers on the desk. Then he took a pair of hornrimmed spectacles out of a drawer and put them on. "I've always been fascinated by mysteries," he said. "It's part of my work, I suppose. This may take a little time."

He went around the desk, pulled a chair out from behind it, and laid the manuscript down in front of him. He bent over it, slowly turning the pages. I sipped my tea and waited.

The flat was somewhere at the back of the building. There was no noise of traffic. It was very quiet. Faintly, I could hear the children in the next room squabbling over their game, and their mother trying to shut them up. I looked at the books near me. Most of them were reference works concerned with his calling, but there was also a shelf of modern novels. I pulled out one, a Mary McCarthy and began to turn over the pages silently.

Eventually he sighed, sat back, and closed the book. "No," he said. "I'm sorry to disappoint you but it's just what it pretends to be—a modern imitation of an ancient illuminated manuscript Gospel. So far as I can see, and I've been through it pretty thoroughly, there's not a word or a sentence astray."

I felt as if I'd been kicked in the stomach. We were right back in square one. It had all been for nothing.

"Do you mind my asking," his voice went on, "whose work it is?"

"Not a bit. A man called Eamon O'Beirne."

"O'Beirne? You know I thought I recognized the touch. I've seen some of his work before. It's very fine. If you bury this, Mr. Graham, in another thousand years or so when someone digs it up, it will be priceless."

"It's a little long to wait."

"Perhaps. He's an Irishman, isn't he? I remember meeting him in the museum. He came in to consult us once or twice. How is he?"

"He's dead."

"Dead! But, good heavens, he was a young man. How did he die? Oh, yes, I see. . . ." His voice died away. "There doesn't seem to be very much else to say then, does there, Mr. Graham?"

"No," I said, "except to thank you for your help and your time and your tea." I picked the manuscript up and put it back in my bag.

"Where is the cumhdach which this came from?" he asked.

"It's abroad," I said, "in Corsica."

"I see. May I take it this is not a police matter?"

"You may. O'Beirne died abroad, too. You know, you can always check my bona fides with Robin Saunders."

He smiled then. "I did that, Mr. Graham, before you came. Perhaps I was leading you on a little. As I told you, I've always loved mysteries. In the meantime, however, I imagine I must de-

142

cide to put all recollection of your visit quite out of my mind. Would that be discreet?"

"Very discreet," I said, and I held out my hand. "I think you must be a very good examiner, Mr. Browne. I'll just add one thing."

"And what is that?"

"I give you full marks for this interview."

A cruising taxi was going by as I left the flats. I hailed it and told the driver the address of my club. In my room I took out the manuscript and went through it page by page. The two pages at the end were blank, as Browne had said, but I hardly thought that O'Beirne was simple enough to trust his secret to invisible ink. Still, if nothing else came up, I supposed I'd have to have them tested. Although I accepted entirely what Browne had told me, I still believed that the secret was buried somewhere in the book. After all, O'Beirne had said so urgently in his dying words. And every other single thing that had happened pointed to this answer. Yet, if the secret was here, where was it?

I examined the thick leaves to see if they could have in some way been stuck together to form a receptacle for a letter between them. But even a quick look told me that was impossible. Then I stared at the brilliant lettering, wondering if O'Beirne could have adapted the Irish wording of the Gospel into a code. If he had, then neither I nor anyone else was likely to find the key to it. I smoked three cigarettes, staring at the meaningless, beautiful lettering until it began to jump in front of my eyes. Then I shut the book in despair and went downstairs.

I badly needed a drink. To get to the bar I had to cross the reading room. Near the door a member was sitting in an armchair, his face hidden behind the *Financial Times*.

As I approached him, he put down the paper. "Ah, my dear fellow," he said, "care to join me for a drink?" It was Charles Coningsby Manahan.

18

Un Deserteur

"Manahan!" I said. "How the devil did you get in here?"

"Really, my dear chap, rather a tactless question, don't you think? You didn't know, perhaps, that I am a member of the club in Dublin? We have a reciprocal arrangement here. Oh, yes, I've been a member there now for several years. I was proposed by a lord and seconded by a steward. Admittedly the lord was not a very good one and owed me a lot of money and I had gotten the steward's daughter out of a very embarrassing situation. But that's the way things go nowadays, isn't it? Do come along."

In the bar he ordered whiskey and soda for me and vodka and lime juice for himself. It was typical of him, I thought, to have that preposterous drink.

"You didn't keep our last appointment," I said.

"Something turned up quite unexpectedly. Well, perhaps not quite unexpectedly, but enough to detain me."

"Oh, what?"

"I'm going to put my cards on the table with you, Graham. I've decided that in dealing with you it's the best way." He looked me straight in the eyes.

I knew very well that when he talked about putting his cards on the table and gave me that level stare he was up to something particularly nasty. It was a ploy to impress clients or to bluff an opposing solicitor into an unfavorable settlement. It was very well done, too. There was a carefully contrived expression of sincerity and good faith on his features. If you hadn't known him for what he was, you'd have opened your closet and let him see the skeletons, given him your bank account, and told him all about your wife. No wonder he had the wealth and beauty and talent and nobility of Ireland in his waiting room.

"All right," I said, "let's see your hand."

"I went to Corsica the other day, just before we met at Edgar's party, much against my wishes, to safeguard an investment. Someone wrote me that Edgar was becoming more and more irresponsible and irrational. The evening of the party he had an attack—a proper one. He has paresis."

"How does a queer get that?"

"I don't think we need bother about the techniques of deviation. But I want you to know that I was, in fact, very anxious to see you that night to discuss matters. Then Edgar's illness blew up in my face. I still wanted to talk to you. I sent the Contessa to try to get you to come to the Casa d'Oro. It didn't work out it seems."

"It did not. She brought her strong-arm man along in case her charms were insufficient."

Again he gave me that Honest John look straight between the eyes. "She's afraid of you, Graham," he said.

"She has a strange way of showing it then."

"It's true. You see, I know your type very well. After all, I should. I've acted for lots of them and dealt with them one way or another for years. Basically, you and your like are violent men. You're the leftover remains of a warrior caste. In peacetime you sublimate the itch for violence in dangerous activity like riding races and trying to break your own necks or anyone else's who gets between you and the rails. But the itch is there all the time. You're conditioned to it from childhood. Two

145

wars have thinned your ranks, but they've toughened those who are left into a sort of disregard for any rules but those of class and caste."

"This is quite a sermon," I said. "I hardly expected it from you."

"The subject has always fascinated me ever since I started practice and had to learn the hard way how to deal with you. You're as extinct as the mastodon and the dinosaur if you only knew it. You and Herald and the rest of you, the gentlemen killers, the upper-class toughs, to whom guns come as handy as walking sticks—you belong to history now, along with the Knights of the Round Table. Your place has been taken by faceless misfits who have never been to public schools, who are so sorry for themselves that they want to take it out on everyone else, who haven't any rules at all, who aren't afraid to run when they have to, who loathe violence and only employ it as a last resort and then use knives and blow guns and poison pistols, things you wouldn't call at all nice. They're modern men, Graham, not aging monsters, and I'm one of them. I detest violence."

"For a man who can say that, you seem to be doing pretty well. What about the truck that tried to sideswipe us coming back from Propriano? What about the gunman in Ireland?"

"The truck was all Edgar's idea. I was horrified when I heard about it. So was the Contessa."

"She was, was she? She was on the truck. I saw her."

"She tried to stop them. Thinking back, I believe in this instance we may have been wrong and Edgar right. Had that particular act of violence succeeded, you would have all been killed, no questions would have been asked, and we wouldn't have this trouble on our hands. But Edgar was already suffering from *folie de grandeur*. It's a symptom of that illness, you know. It started, I think, if only we'd recognized it, with that nonsense about having his racing colors on his vehicles, then he had to buy a stud in Ireland and have his colors carried again. Admittedly I was not in a position to oppose that particular pur-

146

chase, since I was acting for the Vendor as well. The Duke of Leix and Offaly—you may know him perhaps. No? He ran into a little trouble with the locals and had to sell up. He was a bit too uninhibited in his habits for rural Ireland. The Garda Siochanu, so he told me, have very little sense of humor or appreciation of youthful masculine beauty. It was all very suitable. He and Edgar had the same tastes and knew each other. They had met in Mexico. I was able to arrange the deal with the minimum of trouble and, I must confess, did quite well out of it. The Duke actually agreed to pay me a most handsome portion of the purchase money, which I put down as a negotiation fee. Rather apt, I thought. Then Edgar found the cumhdach on the place—he took it over lock, stock, and barrel, don't you know. The thing fascinated him and he brought it to Corsica; then, of course, he had to get O'Beirne out to finish it off with an illuminated Gospel. I don't quite know whether he intended to show it to his visitors as a genuine article or not. I suppose he did. More *folie de grandeur,* had we recognized it at the time. You have the cumhdach now, by the way?"

I ignored that innocent and simple-seeming question dropped so easily at the end of his speech. "And the little plan to murder me by medicine at Ballymere?" I asked him.

"You didn't take that seriously? We were only trying to frighten you. Oddly enough, Graham, after practising it for over twenty years I've come to have some respect for the rule of law."

"Provided it doesn't conflict with your own ends."

"Perhaps, but it was I who thought of putting peaceful pressure on through Marston, a plan which you wrecked, let me remind you."

"I thought I saw your fine Italian hand in it somewhere. You know, had you gone on with that, the Contessa would have been in trouble too."

"I scarcely think she knows or cares enough about racing to mind."

"I'll go along with you there. Her interests are in other sports."

"Since I have naturally some experience in handling settlements and the like, I decided to come and see you myself. Can we reach agreement over this thing?"

"Just what do you want?"

"I know you have found the cumhdach. Let's make that common case, shall we?"

"If you like."

"Very well then. I want the answer to three questions. First, where did you go today?"

"Really, Manahan, you're slipping, aren't you? If you've taken all the trouble to come over after me, I should have thought you'd at least have arranged to have me followed and my movements checked."

"Oh, I did. Dont underestimate me. Actually I was myself in the taxi that tailed you. Unfortunately we were rammed from behind by a Jaguar at Hammersmith Broadway. There will be a civil action, of course, and I shall be interested, to say the least of it, to see who the owner of the Jaguar is. Of course we lost you. Fortunately, I remembered you were a member here. A phone call to the porter told me you were expected. I came along and waited."

I smiled to myself as I thought of the accident. So I was being watched and I was getting some active, if unobtrusive, help.

"And the second?" I asked him.

"This is really rather important. I want to know just what was in the cumhdach."

"Third?"

"It follows from the last. If, as I asume, there was a manuscript in the cumhdach I want to know what O'Beirne put into it."

"Are you trying to buy me again?"

He hesitated for a moment, then he said, "Let us put it in this manner: I'm offering you life insurance."

"In just what way?"

"You have to return to Corsica, you know, whether you want to or not."

148

It was my turn to be surprised. "What on earth do you mean?"

"You're a material witness in a murder case."

"How the devil do you know that?"

"I took the liberty of interviewing the British consul after your friends had seen him. He was in rather a state, I may say. Very disturbing to have a murder dropped on your doorstep and with all sorts of conflicting interests of your nationals involved. I gathered, however, that you will have to swear information against McKee, or whatever it is one does to bring the matter before the Juge d'Instruction. I'm not really familiar with the practice in French Courts. But that's roughly it. After I left the consul I hired a light airplane to fly me to Nice, just caught a London plane and arrived in nice time to keep an eye on you."

"If I don't answer the questions?"

"Then, my friend, the matter will be out of my hands forever and into those of the real experts in violence."

"I see. And who are they?"

"If you aren't playing the idiot boy, and I think you are, the answer is that I can't tell you. They're clients. It's a professional secret. But you'll find out soon enough."

"I think you're in trouble yourself over this, Manahan, and you're trying to save your own skin. You said you were putting your cards on the table. All right, here are some of mine. I don't believe you and I don't trust you. You can go to hell."

He put his glass down on the bar with a little thump. Then he got to his feet. "Good-bye, Graham," he said.

I finished my drink. Then I went upstairs to my room. With someone like Manahan floating around, I thought I should mount personal guard over the manuscript.

Picking up the telephone, I told them to send some cold chicken and tongue and half a bottle of Riesling up to me. Then I took the manuscript out of my bag and looked at it.

I ate my meal with it propped up on the bed in front of me. I turned the pages and stared at the beautiful, incomprehensible lettering. I lifted it and turned it over and over in my hands.

149

If you look at an object long enough every detail becomes engraved in your mind. As I stared and wondered, gradually something about the bulk of the thing began to bother me. At first I couldn't make out what it was. Then, as I opened and closed it, lifted it and put it down, my attention began to focus on one part of it. With a sudden quickening of excitement I realized what had caught and held my eye.

The stiff cover of the back was fractionally thicker than the front.

Taking a knife from the table I heated it in the electric fire. Then I gently eased up a corner of the manilla binding and slid the blade underneath. The warmth of the knife melted the glue; inch by inch the paper came away from the boards. I held my breath.

When it was all removed, the edge of the board was revealed. Down the center of it, from top to bottom, very straight and regular, was a thin, hair line crack. I heated the knife again and laid it lengthways along the crack. Then I pressed it home. The two sides came apart. Lying between them was a thin sheet of India paper. I picked it up.

O'Beirne had stretched his cleverness as far as it would go. This must have been a sort of double bluff. He had guessed that if anyone suspected him of having hidden his secret they would be sure they could find it in the text. Therefore he had written a true translation of the Gospel in Irish so that anyone examining it would scratch their heads and finally go away satisfied. Here, in the binding, he had hidden the truth.

The paper was the thinnest and finest available, scarcely more substantial than a gossamer veil. It was covered with minute, accurate copperplate script. And it wasn't in Irish, I noticed thankfully.

Taking it over toward the window, I sat in the easy chair and read it, slowly and carefully, word for word. When I had finished I laid it down, appalled. Then I read it again. Here, if what it said was true, and I had no reason to doubt it, were lunacy and wickedness on a terrifying scale. No wonder he could blackmail them; no wonder they were frightened; no wonder those for whom they were working were ready and willing to kill.

I picked up the telephone and put a call through to Deforge's number in Ajaccio. After a bit they told me he was not available. Then I tried the Bastia number. The answer was the same. It was odd and worrying. Could it be that things were blowing up sooner than had been expected? One thing upon which O'Beirne's memorandum was silent was the date. He hadn't been able to get that, naturally enough, for it was unlikely that Shanks or anyone else in the Casa d'Oro had been entrusted with it. Except perhaps one, the man upstairs who had coughed and whose chair had creaked. I knew who he was now.

On an impulse I picked up the phone once more and rang the hall porter.

"Mr. Manahan, the Irish gentleman, sir?" he said in answer to my query. "He wasn't staying, sir. When he left he told me to get him a taxi."

"You don't remember where he said he was going?"

"I think he told the driver to take him to the airport, sir."

"I see." I put the telephone down. There was nothing much else to be done for the moment. He had twelve hours start on me, whatever use he intended to make of it. I went to bed.

In the morning I read once more the writing on the flimsy paper and memorized it. Then I put it back in its place and re-sealed the binding as best I could. With the assistance of the porter I wrapped the whole thing up in brown paper and string. After that I drove to my bank and deposited it. If anything happened to me no doubt it would be found amongst my effects. It would be an interesting historical document if nothing else. Then I, too, made my way to the airport.

A Trident took me to Nice. There were a couple of hours to wait for the afternoon plane to Ajaccio. I went along to the telephones and once again tried Deforge's number. The operator told me there was *une attente indéterminée* on all calls to Corsica and she didn't know why.

Evil forebodings began to catch hold of me. At the newsstand I bought three French papers. In them at any rate there was no unusual news from Corsica, and search them as I did, item by item, I learned nothing. Or so I thought until I came to an inside page of *Nice-Matin*. It was tucked away down at the bottom right-hand corner.

AJACCIO CORSE

Last night there was a collision on the Col de Cortone near Coti-Chivari between a private car and a camion of the Légion Entrangere. The automobile left the road, fell some distance, and caught fire. It is believed that the driver was killed instantly. Both occupants of the camion were unhurt. The dead man has been identified as M. Jacques Deforge of 34 Rue Jerome, Ajaccio, an import and export agent.

I put down the paper and a wave of sickness welled up into my throat. What did I do now? Deforge might or might not have been an efficient agent. The fact that he was dead probably proved he wasn't. Through him, nevertheless, had lain my only contact with the authorities; through him, too—and I had to face it—had lain my only hope of not being declared a stateless person for the rest of my life. Deforge was now dead and I was left with the secret, carefully memorized, he and the rest of them had been searching for. Could I go to the authorities here?

The English were more than likely to kick me off the doorstep straight away as an undesirable. In any case, they wouldn't want to get mixed up in this unofficially, and before doing anything through official channels they would require such a mass of requisitions in triplicate and checking and cross-checking that it would be at least a month until any move was made. The French, on the other hand, were more than likely to regard me as an Albion out to make trouble, or else barking mad. If only I knew who was in the business here in Nice. There must be someone who kept contact with Deforge, and if I could reach him things might move him in time. Unfortunately, I'd no idea who he was.

At that moment the speaker crackled announcing my flight to Ajaccio. There didn't seem anything else to do but to go along. I had to see the British consul anyway. Perhaps he would listen to me. Perhaps. It appeared a pretty slim hope. I felt naked, defenceless, and sick. Simon had said I had gotten myself into a pretty mess. He could say that again, in spades. I went along to the metropolitan departure lounge and took my place in the queue.

We came into Ajaccio airport on a tilting, banking approach over the bay and inside the ring of mountains. I spared a moment to think that this must be no fun for the pilot or anyone else in bad weather. Then we were down. I collected my bag from the moving track and walked out into the sun.

They were all around me before I knew what was happening. Very smart and efficient they were, with their pipe-clayed webbing and anklets, their PM armbands, and their white kepis. In an instant two of them had me by the shoulders and were frogmarching me toward a brown Foreign Legion camion with a canvas cover drawn up beside the airport entrance. Those photographs taken in Casa d'Oro must have provided all the identification they wanted, I thought inconsequentially.

I struggled like hell, for all the good it did me. Someone hit me a wallop on the side of my head. Another had my arm up behind me in a grip I knew. It hurt.

"*Un déserteur,*" I heard the sergeant explain to bystanders. Then I was flung into the back of the camion with two of them on top of me.

My wrists were jerked back behind me. I felt something being put around them and pulled tight. The engine started.

The camion moved off down the airport road. The webbing strap round my wrists was pulled tighter and secured with a click. I was slammed back into a sitting position against the driver's partition. My head sang. I wondered what had really happened to Deforge before he died. He must have talked. These chaps were experts. They had learned the job in Algeria. I didn't blame him.

19

Remember an Inn?

It's a mistake, of course, to think, as some civilized people still do, that torture went out with the Middle Ages. Every security force since then has used it to obtain the information it requires. I was under no illusions as to what was going to happen to me. Nor had I any doubt that they could make me talk, too— in time. At the top of the rise in the road we turned sharply to the right. The camion trundled along at a good pace, crossed the bridge over the Prunelli River, and took the road into the hills. That meant, I thought, that we were making for Bonifacio. I remembered Simon telling me of the Legion depot there in the tiny mysterious walled town perched on a great cliff at the end of the island. The barracks was built right on the edge of that cliff, overlooking the narrow entrance to the harbor. Beneath it was a honeycomb of ancient and modern galleries. There were gun and searchlight emplacements and there were also old oubliettes diving down under the surface of the sea from which the sad and broken bodies of victims could be slid, weighted, into forty fathoms of water and never return to the surface. It was not a cheering prospect.

I looked at the man next to me. He was a Singhalese with a
154

peculiar circular scar on his cheek. He belched and picked his nose. The man opposite was a hulking big brute, probably a Teuton. Without taking his eyes from my face he got a package of chewing gum from his pocket, stripped the wrappings away, and put it into his mouth. In the back a third, a gangling youth, propped himself as best he could against the swaying of the truck. The sergeant, I supposed, was up front with the driver.

We went on, making pretty good time over the twisting roads.

Suddenly a horn blared and blared again behind us. Above the tailboard I saw a flash of white as a car crowded past us. Then the camion began to grind to a stop. It pulled up. There was the sound of a door slamming as someone got down from in front. A moment or two later there came the noise of voices raised in dispute. They came nearer. The sergeant was being told to do something he didn't like, and was saying so in no uncertain terms. The other voice was a woman's. I had no difficulty at all in recognizing it. It belonged to the Contessa.

They stopped opposite the end of the truck and the argument went on.

Then the Contessa said flatly, "Those are my father's orders. You may know that he does not take kindly to being disobeyed."

The sergeant came around the end of the camion. He in turn barked an order. He looked thunderous.

The two men near me got up and took hold of me. I was manhandled down from the truck and over the tailboard. I landed on the road blinking in the sun. I stumbled, swayed, and just kept on my feet. The Military Police looked as if they'd have been a great deal more pleased if I hadn't.

The Contessa was standing a few yards away. Her arms were on her hips and she was looking at the sergeant. She was wearing her jeans and a red shirt. She said something I didn't catch and emphasized it with a jerk of her hand.

The white Alfa was drawn up just beyond the camion. The sergeant gave another order. The two M.P.'s took my arms and

155

marched me toward the Alfa. The chap with the cicatrice got the point of his elbow into my kidneys as a sort of farewell gesture. I looked at him. "I'll remember you, *cochon,*" I said.

The other helped me along with his knee under the base of my spine, catching me before I could fall. They both laughed. One of them opened the door of the car and they pushed me inside.

The Contessa came behind with the sergeant. She went around to the driver's door and stood by it for a second, looking at him. Some sort of silent struggle took place between them. Then he drew himself to attention and his hand came up in a salute. She nodded and got in beside me.

Her hand went to the ignition key. The car came to life. She started to drive, very fast, around the corners and into the hills.

"Nice to see you again, Contessa," I said. "And just where are we off to now?"

She didn't answer. I strained at my bonds. They held.

Some miles further along we left the main road for a minor one. A few minutes later we again turned aside into a still lesser road whose surface was pitted with rocky outcrops and huge yawning holes. This slowed our progress. We were climbing all the time. Sometimes, as the road turned back on itself, I caught the flash of the sea far below.

After a little while we came to the head of the pass. Set back some way from the crest with a screen of chestnut trees and cork oaks around it was a square, dingy building. In front of it were one or two battered iron tables and chairs. Hens scrabbled about and somewhere a dog barked. In fading, flaking black letters on the wall facing us was the word AUBERGE.

The Contessa drove around it into a small yard. Here were more signs of dilapidation and neglect. Tiles were off the sagging roofs, doors hung awry on their hinges, paint had not been applied to anything for years. She ran the car into an open shed beside an ancient bullock cart. Switching off the engine, she turned to me.

"The man who owns this place," she said, "fought against the British in Syria under my father. He was wounded twice, the second time in the stomach. It has left him with a permanent injury. He does not like your nation."

"Just who is your father?"

"He was General Celle. He died last night."

I whistled. "That may make things awkward for a lot of people," I said. "Does anyone know of this?"

"Three of us. Now get out of the car."

"I find that rather difficult with my hands bound. I think it's only a piece of web equipment. Undo it, will you?"

She smiled. "I may have something else to help you." She reached behind her and picked up her handbag. Opening it she showed me the little Browning inside. "I will use it if I must," she said.

"I always did think women and guns a very dangerous combination. Since I've known you, I've had no reason to change my mind. All right. Open the door."

I put my legs to the ground and pushed myself upright. We were pretty high in the mountains here, I imagined. The air was thin and almost cold.

"Go in through that door," she said, "and don't try any tricks, Graham. I will use this, you know. The patron will help me, too."

He was waiting for us, a little brown man who surveyed me with an unfriendly glance. His eyes were bloodshot and he had the bad color of the stomach sufferer. He led us up a flight of worn stone stairs and showed us into a big, airy, corner room. One of its windows, I noticed, commanded the way we had come.

There was a wooden floor, a rough deal table, a couple of wicker chairs, a wide bed, and a deal wardrobe.

"Would M'sieu like some cognac?" she asked me mockingly. "M'sieu must have had a trying experience."

I sat down in one of the wicker chairs. I was aching from my beating up. "Come to think of it, I would and I have," I said.

The little man went off. He was back in a few minutes with a tray on which were two glasses, a bottle of brandy, and a bottle of Orezza. He poured two man-sized slugs into the glasses, recorked the bottle, opened the Orezza with a quick flip of his hand and left us.

"Just how am I supposed to drink this?" I asked her.

She took the little gun out of her bag and went around behind my chair. I felt her fingers working at my bonds. The catch opened and the strap loosened. She came in front of me, facing me. The gun was remarkably steady in her hand. She was just too far away for me to jump her. She probably knew that. Anyway, the pain of circulation coming back put that out of my mind for the moment.

When I could again use my fingers, or some of them, I poured Orezza into both the glasses and pushed one over toward her.

"Well," I said, looking at her and lifting my glass, "as I may have said before, you're a rotten little bitch, but even in those clothes you're a very lovely woman, in case you don't know. But of course you do know. Just what are you up to now?"

"Among other things, Graham, I'm saving you from yourself."

"I might believe that if you'd put that gun away."

She looked at me and then down at the gun in her hand. She hesitated a moment and then appeared to make up her mind. She gave a little laugh and her hand moved. The gun described a small arc and landed on the bed beside my chair.

20

Two of a Kind

It lay there within easy reach, gleaming and wicked and lethal. I made no move to pick it up. She raised her glass and drank, looking at me over its rim.

"Your call, Graham, I think," she said.

"So it's not loaded after all," I said.

"Why not look and see?"

I did pick it up then. I pulled back the action. There was a round in the breech and a full clip in the magazine. I put it down beside me. Who knew, it might come in useful yet.

"General Celle," I said, "the legendary hero of Morocco. He was the man upstairs in the Casa d'Oro. He was the figurehead of the whole affair. O'Beirne knew that. And you're his daughter."

"Yes."

"Just for the record, was there ever a Count?"

"Not so far as I know. It was another of Edgar's grandiose ideas."

"I didn't really imagine there was, but I never got around to looking it up. For that matter where does one get hold of an Almanach de Gotha nowadays. There isn't one in my club."

"My father's lungs and his heart were damaged in Indochina. He was an old man and old men are easy prey to delusions. He was a regular soldier. He served France. Ever since 1941 he has disliked and distrusted the General. It was inevitable, I think, for him to have regarded the Algerian settlement as a betrayal and to have thrown in his lot with the colons. After the surrender we had to leave on the run—Spain, Switzerland, Greece, the strain of constant traveling, of being hunted and disgraced told on his health. It was one of the reasons we persuaded him to accept Edgar's offer of rest and hospitality."

"We?"

"My mother died just before we left Greece. I suppose you can die of a broken heart. I don't know. After we left Algeria, she just faded away from worry and strain. She only wanted one thing—for him to end his days in peace and comfort. She loved him, you see. So did I."

"I suppose it was Manahan who made the contact?"

"Yes. He was in a yacht cruising in the Greek Islands, probably with that aim in view. I don't know. One never knows with Charles. He keeps himself in the background and pulls the strings. He and Edgar have worked together for years, but Edgar was really only, what do you call it, the front man. Charles was always the brains of the outfit. It was he who set Edgar up here. They started off innocently enough, buying up land for development, operating the fishing concession, and doing a bit of smuggling on the side. Then during the Algerian troubles they either got the idea themselves or were approached by the O.A.S. I don't know. Does it matter? O'Beirne found it all out.

"I suppose he put it down."

"Oh, yes. Most of it anyway. I don't think he realized that Manahan was the boss. He seemed to think it was Shanks who had built up the organization for getting wanted men out of Algeria and hiding them. He looked after their leaders and entertained them, especially when they were on the run. Gradually the thing grew and he became the custodian of their secrets and their funds. The colons who are resettled all along the east coast have been using the Casa d'Oro as a headquarters and clearing house for all their dreams of revenge and return.

160

Shanks—and Manahan, of course—were well, indeed munificently, paid. No wonder they were frightened when O'Beirne started to blackmail them. No wonder they were prepared to safeguard their investment right up to murder and beyond."

She shivered and her glance went involuntarily to the window, as if expecting danger. All at once a chill seemed to come into the room. The chill of fear, perhaps. "It goes further than that," she said.

"I know it does. O'Beirne knew. He learned a lot, O'Beirne, but he hadn't learned how to keep himself alive."

"What did he know besides what you've said?"

"He found out that a plot was being hatched—a lunatic, murderous, fanatic plot such as can only come to life in the minds of the dispossessed. Your father may have been old and sick and dying, but he was concerned in that plot. He was its justification to the world, its stamp of respectability."

"Well, what if he was?" she flared at me suddenly. "You smug English who never fight for your honor, who slide away from your responsibilities mouthing platitudes about the wind of change, you've never been outlawed. You've been too clever for that. You cannot understand."

"I think a good many of us can understand very well. I think the Kenya settlers know just how you and your like feel. But they've had the sense to see that this sort of murderous lunacy only makes things worse. And it is murderous lunacy, and you know it. It can't hope to succeed."

"That's what *he* thinks. Do you know what *he* said in '61? *Ce qui est grave dans cette affaire, Messieurs, c'est qu'elle n'est pas sérieux.* He is older and weaker now and they are stronger than they were then. He has no one to succeed him. His self-confidence can cost him his life and destroy France."

"How?"

"Because, don't you see, they have a base now here in Corsica. Before they had to make a futile attempt at a landing. Now they are established. They have a civilian population, the transplanted colons, behind them. The eastern half of the island is theirs for the taking. And they have an army—or part of one."

161

"The Legion. That must be the maddest idea of the lot. They didn't come out before. They won't now."

"Not all. Not at first, anyhow. But don't you see what is happening? It's Gregorov, the Colonel you met."

"What about him?"

"He's besotted with hatred for what he calls the betrayal of the Legion. He fought at Dien Bien Phu. He had never forgotten Indochina or forgiven the government for it. He escaped the purges after the last revolt. His friends covered up for him and he was one of those they missed. He has gone on working. He has kept in touch with the leaders of the deserters who went over to the O.A.S., the discontented paras, the murder gangs. Now he has brought them back. They're at the Casa d'Oro in Legion uniforms—most of them. Some are lying low in sympathizers' houses in Bonifacio. More are in a hotel near Corte owned by an ex-colon. There is a Legion battle exercise with live ammunition starting tomorrow for two days. He has arranged to put his killers into it alongside one or two battalions where they have managed to make converts. They will be ready to go the following morning—do you know what day that is?"

"July 14th, Bastille Day!"

"Exactly. And that is when they will strike."

"Have they tied in anything else? O'Beirne was short on dates, though he seems to have gotten the outline right. He thought they would aim at the heart as well, but he couldn't find out much about that part of the plan."

"He was right. They will assassinate him."

"They've tried before and failed."

"This time they will succeed. When they do, there are those who think as they do waiting to seize power. Who else is there who can govern?"

"I see. How did your father die?"

"He killed himself. He was only a dupe, a cat's-paw to be flung aside when once he had served his purpose. It wasn't until the very end that he realized it. They told him only what they wanted him to know. Then Gregorov became openly contemptuous and insolent. His eyes were opened at last and he saw

162

that it was personal ambition, greed, madness, and treachery that was driving them on. When he discovered that the house he was living in was also concealing a gang of deserters and murderers he finally made up his mind to have done with it all. He had kept one of those pills from his days in Indochina. I was with him when he took it. He told me it cost him hardly a moment's thought. He had little of life left and nothing of anything else."

She took a cigarette from a package on the table and walked away from me toward the windows. I watched her light the cigarette and draw on it.

"Why are you telling me all this?" I asked her quietly.

"Don't you see? I always hated them. I hated them more than I believed a human being could hate for what they were doing to my father. It was he I was always trying to protect and help. He had suffered enough. It was he I was working for, lying for, doing what I hated and despised. I was wrong. We both were, my mother and I, we should have left him to die in Greece. At least he would have died there with his honor intact. When he killed himself, I was free."

"Why rescue me?"

She looked away. "I thought I owed you something," she said slowly.

Perhaps she did, too, but I doubted if that was her only motive. I finished my brandy and poured myself some more. "Where do we go from here?" I asked her.

"We must stay where we are. No one will find us."

"You said only three people knew your father was dead. Who are they?"

"Manahan, myself, and you."

"Shanks?"

"He doesn't matter any more. He's in a dark room shot full of drugs."

"What is Manahan doing about it all?"

"I don't know. He has an instinct for survival, I think. I'm sure it was always his intention to slip away before the shooting started. He wouldn't have been here at all if it hadn't been for Edgar's going mad. There'll be money deposited for Charles in

163

a Swiss bank. If they succeed, there will be more. If they fail, he'll have the money and his development lands over here. He'll be no worse off."

"That's how he likes to play it all right. He wants to bet on a million to nothing. And Gregorov, does he know?"

"He must by now, I suppose."

"Is he a genuine fanatic or an agent provocateur?"

"I don't know. It comes to the same thing in the end, doesn't it? This thing could split the West."

"Do you want to stop it?" I said.

"Yes. But what can we do?"

"We must get out. We've wasted enough time hanging around as it is. We've got to get into Ajaccio and warn someone. That is, if anyone will listen to us."

She stubbed out her cigarette. "No," she said.

"Just what is going on in that scheming little mind of yours now?"

"Gregorov must know about us by now. He has always distrusted me. It was just a chance I reached that truck before the news came through. You saw how suspicious the sergeant was. He probably telephoned to say what had happened as soon as he could reach a line. They'll have every road—there are only a few of them anyway—watched for us."

"Then we'll have to take to the hills and walk."

"Do you think we'd have a chance over this country at night? You must have seen enough of it to know you wouldn't go a mile without being lost or falling over a cliff edge. Don't be a fool, Graham."

"So here we stay like fish in a barrel waiting to be shot. Now tell me in plain language what you are up to, Contessa?"

"No one knows this place."

"That's what O'Beirne thought and look what happened to him."

She put her hands on the table and looked steadily at me. "Before I left," she said, "I sent a messenger I could trust to your friend Simon Herald. I told him you were with me. I
164

also told him as much as I dared of what was happening and that he had to get to Ajaccio and warn the authorities. I said it was the only way of saving your life."

"When did you send that message?"

She hesitated, then she said, "Before I left the Casa d'Oro."

"Before you did your little act with the sergeant and fished me out of the camion?"

"Yes."

"Very clever, Contessa. Very clever indeed. I congratulate you. You wanted me as bait, didn't you? That's why you had to go to the trouble and risk to get me free. I didn't think it was all for the sake of my bright eyes somehow. You knew Simon wouldn't do anything to help you, that he'd see you damned first. But, being the man he is, you reckoned he'd go through hell and high water to get his old school chum, Graham, out of a mess. That was it, wasn't it?"

She looked at me defiantly. "Where else could I turn?" she said. "It was the only chance we had."

"Well, I'll tell you something, Contessa. The last time we met, Simon and I had a flaming row. He threw me out of the house and told me not to come back. Being the man he is, do you know what he's likely to say now, when he gets that message? 'Let him rot,' that's what he'll say. You might have had some hope if you'd sent the message to his wife."

"That insipid little creature. I suppose she's in love with you."

"As a matter of fact she's not. She's one of those strange women who are in love with their husbands. There aren't many around these days, I know, but she's one of them."

Suddenly she looked young and frightened. I poured her another slug of brandy and pushed the glass across the table toward her. "We're lost then," she said.

"No. Not quite, so long as we have ourselves, some brandy, and a gun. Drink up. Come on. Here's to us. There's none like us. By God, it's true in your case anyway!"

She lifted the glass. Whatever else she had or had not she had too much guts to remain downcast for long. She laughed and drank. "If I had to be lost I'm glad it's with you, Graham," she said.

"Where do these maneuvers start?"

"I don't know. Not far away, I think. We're in the area."

"We'll try to get through at first light tomorrow morning," I said.

She came around the table and stood beside me. "Do you still hate me, Graham?" she asked.

"The trouble is I don't hate you at all, you lying little bitch." I took her shoulders and pulled her toward me. She came willingly, urgently. Her body was young and firm and demanding. Her arms went around my neck. "This is what I've longed for ever since that afternoon in the hills. You've known that," I said.

"Of course I've known it. And what do you think I've wanted, Graham?"

I picked her up.

"Love me a little, Graham," she said. And again, "Love me a little."

Later she stirred in my arms and woke. She whispered mockingly to me in the darkness, "I could hardly have let you be broken by the Legion thugs before this had happened, could I, Graham?" Then her questing fingers found and traced my recent wounds. "Bullet scars," she said, "new ones. I think you live a lie too, Graham. Gentleman adventurer indeed. That's what Manahan said you were, and I told him he was right. But he wasn't quite clever enough. I knew better. We used to call them Barbouzes in Algeria, Graham. Do you know what they did to them?"

"Yes."

"It wouldn't have done, Graham, before we had this together, would it? We're two of a kind, dear Graham. Always remember that." She caught and pulled me to her again.

21

From a View

A peculiar clattering sound awoke me. The big room was flooded with sunlight. The sun was far higher than we should have allowed it to be before starting on our journey. I slid out of bed and went to the window. The clattering grew louder and louder. Then an army helicopter came over the mountain crest very low, and went crabwise along the road. It was so low I could see the occupants. Involuntarily I took a step backward into the room. She murmured something and turned in her sleep. The clattering went away and then came back, as the helicopter turned in its tracks. This time it was right down at rooftop height. I could see the crew peering at the yard and the windows of the inn.

I looked at the bed. She stirred again but did not waken. Her passion had had an intensity which almost frightened me. It had been demanding and yet at the same time despairing. She was very lovely against the pillows, her hair framing the little heart-shaped face from which sleep and fulfillment had removed the lines of strain and fear.

I went toward the other window to follow the helicopter's course. It clattered down into the valley below. As I watched, I saw, right at the bottom of the pass, a big brown camion of the

Legion appear around the first hairpin bends and come to a halt. Men in camouflage denims spilled out of it and began to file in battle order up the road. I was across the room in two strides.

"Wake up," I said, taking her by the shoulder and shaking it. "Get some clothes on and quickly. There's a platoon of the Legion at the bottom of the pass."

She came awake, slowly at first and then more rapidly, as awareness banished dreams. "What's happening?" she said drowsily.

"I'm not sure. But the two-day scheme seems to have started. Simon the Marines. We're on our own."

"I thought I heard something . . ."

"That was a helicopter looking in our windows. I don't know whether they're on to us or not. Either way, we've got to get out. Hurry up. Here." I threw the jeans on the bed. "Can we get to Ajaccio from this place?"

"There's a way around through the mountains by Viconza. But they'll have the roads blocked . . ."

"We'll go as far as we can in the car and then try it on foot. That's our only chance."

She pulled up a zip. "It's a long journey," she said. "And that white car can be seen for miles."

"Have you any better ideas?"

"No. Do you have to be so rotten?"

"It's only because I'm frightened. Give me the little gun."

She put her hand under the pillow and held it out to me. "How near are they now?" she said.

I crossed again to the window. I could see the white kepis coming around a curve about a mile down the road; some were in the maquis on either side. "A fairish way," I said. "It must be part of a sweep. I don't believe they know we're here. They're not hurrying. It'll take them a good half-hour to reach us."

"In that case . . ." She sat down before the looking glass, ran a comb through her hair, and began to make up her face.

"For Christ's sake," I said, "what are you doing? Playing Marie Antoinette?"

"I refuse to meet the Legion looking like a *poule de bido* after a thick night."

"You looked more like April Morn a minute or so ago. I'll have to hand it to you. You're General Celle's daughter all right. You've got his guts. But if you don't get away from that dressing table in ten seconds I'll take you by the slack of those pants and make you leave."

"Thank you, Graham. Always the charmer. I'm ready now."

Our rope-soled shoes made no noise on the stone stairs. The rest of the building was silent and the ground floor rooms were dark and shuttered.

She backed the Alfa out of the yard and set it going down the far side of the pass. We entered a long patch of shade between rows of chestnuts.

"I hope there's no another camion coming up this way," I said.

"If we can get down into the valley a road will take us to Viconza in those hills. From there, you can almost see Ajaccio."

Below us the long narrow valley gradually opened out. It's floor was a desolation of rock and burned earth and maquis. Beyond its immediate ridge there rose in grandeur tier after tier of serrated peaks. The sun blazed down. Nothing disturbed the stillness except the noise of our passing. It was silent, savage, and impressive.

She took the little car around the hairpins at the edge of safety. The wheels screamed and scrabbled. I hoped she could hold it if we slid. At first on our left was a sheer drop. This gave place, as we descended, to a tangle of scrub and cork oaks. Around every corner I expected to meet a Legion truck grinding its way up. The little Browning was on my knee. It wasn't exactly the weapon I'd have chosen to take on an armed squad of killers. I glanced at her. Her face was set as she concentrated on the immediate needs of controlling the car. At least she had that to take her mind off our plight.

We got down all right. A signpost at a T-junction pointed left to Viconza. She changed gears for the turning. Almost immediately we were climbing again and rounding more of the interminable hairpins of Corsican mountain roads.

I looked over my shoulder the way we had come. It was just as well I did. Another Legion camion was approaching the T-junction along its farther arm. It seemed as if, on these exposed turns, we were bound to be seen.

"Pull into the far side," I said, "and stop."

"Why?"

"There's another camion down below."

"We can leave him standing."

"And what about the chums he can summon up to head us off? Pull up quickly, dammit. There, look."

We were beside a place where the road-menders had hewn stones and material out of the mountain. It was disused now and mostly overgrown. Obediently she swung the wheel and nosed the white car into it.

A few cork oaks were growing beneath the far edge of the road. Their tops reached high enough to throw shade on the tarred surface and to give me some cover. I told her to stay where she was and crossed over to look.

The camion had stopped at the junction. As I reached the roadside an officer got out. He had a pair of field glasses in his hand. He looked a bit like Gregorov, but at this distance I couldn't be certain. Putting the glasses to his eyes, he began to sweep the surrounding country.

The scar made by our road ran right across the hillside to where a cluster of houses and a notch in the ridge was, I supposed, Viconza. As I watched, the officer began to search the whole length of the road through the glasses. When they came opposite to me, I lay flat behind the little parapet. I thought the car was well enough concealed in the quarry and that the cork oaks would break up his vision. Apparently I was right, for he got back into the camion. It took the turn to the left, up the pass.

I waited until it was out of sight. Then I ran back to her.

"He has gone the way we came," I said. "We've got a head start. But if he questions them at the inn I suppose they'll talk."

While I was speaking she had backed the Alfa out onto the

170

road. It took us another twenty minutes to reach the village. It consisted of a single narrow street with a couple of down-at-the-heel cafés, an alimentation, and a boulangerie. The shops reminded me we hadn't breakfasted. Since we had at any rate a few minutes to spare, I told her to stop. I bought a loaf of bread and a cake, some fruit, and a bottle of wine. We began to eat as we went along.

Once through the cleft in the ridge the western side of the island opened up. Far away to the left I thought I could see a part of the bay and the port installations of Ajaccio. Below and in front, miles away, the sun shone on a gleam of yellow sand and the sea. The road curled down below us, clinging to the side of the hill. The sky was cloudless; a purple haze of heat covered the valleys.

"I don't think he can catch us now," I said. "If you know the way we ought to be home in a hack. Perhaps we should stop and have a picnic."

It was at that moment that I heard the helicopter. It came clattering over the cleft behind us, low down, a huge obscene insect with its plastic tail and dangling skids.

The road was bare of cover. This time there was no quarry into which we could dive. We were caught, pinned, like a fly on a wall. I looked back and above. It had come over the crest and was almost on top of us. It turned aside, crabwise, across the valley.

"How far until the next town?" I asked her.

"It's about twenty miles to Ponto Varicchio."

"Any turnoffs?"

"I don't think so."

"I wonder how soon he can get to his chums."

"What's that?"

There was a staccato burst of firing behind us, followed by another. It was some distance away.

"Nothing. It's not at us, at any rate. They've begun letting off their live ammunition, that's all. Press on. We'll try to make the town before they can get someone after us."

The little car went scudding again around the bends. I didn't

171

have much hope that we were going to get away with this. Twenty miles was too far to travel without interference. Some-one with whom the helicopter could make contact was bound to be nearer than that.

I was right. They were nearer, much nearer. We hadn't gone more than a mile when I saw them below us. There were six of them in camouflage uniforms and carrying automatic weapons. They climbed out of the maquis and onto the road. One of them had a walkie-talkie.

"Crash stop, quick," I said. "We've had it this way."

She slammed her foot on the brake. The car slithered and scrabbled to a standstill. "They've cut the road below us," I told her.

"I see," she said. "Clever Colonel Gregorov. He had the whole area covered. Very well, *mon Général,* what are your orders now?"

"We'll take to the maquis ourselves. It's our only hope."

We had to go back the way we'd come for some distance before we could find a practical place to climb off the road. Then we went up over the rocky surface, pulling ourselves along by young trees and saplings. It was rough going, but at least the cover was fairly good. And, I consoled myself, we were point-ing in the approximate direction of Ajaccio.

At the top of the ridge we paused for breath. Down below on the road I heard a shout. They had found the car.

In front of us was a tangled mass of cork oaks, chestnuts, and maquis. We plunged into this and began to fight our way through. They hadn't seen us yet and we were still under cover. We had a chance of a start while they cast to pick up the trail; I thought of my careless fox-hunting days and began to have considerable sympathy for the fox.

There were a few narrow goat paths through the scrub. We made slow going. Thorn and growing shrubs tore at our clothes and hands as we fought our way along. The leaves and foliage of the trees gave a little shelter from the sun, but it was desper-ately hot.

172

Soon the trees thinned out into isolated patches of oaks and scrub. The going was better, but the cover was less. Then the trees gave way to an open space of rock and stones. Fifty yards away, facing us, a sheer wall of rock reached upward. It was gray and smooth and solid. About thirty feet high and quite unclimbable, it appeared to run right along our front.

"We'll have to try to find a way around," I said. "At least we seem to have lost them for the moment."

I wasn't being very clever in my appreciations that morning. As soon as I finished speaking, I heard the shout.

He had worked around us to the higher ground on our left. From there he could command the open stretch on which we stood. He was signaling with his Sten gun held aloft. He wasn't all that far away. I could see his white kepi quite clearly.

We ran along beside the rock wall. It bore back on itself in a curve, and then it suddenly stopped. It stopped all right. At our feet was an abyss going down into the misty depths of another great valley.

There were more shouts behind us now. The hounds were closing in. Looking back, I saw them clear of cover, their numbers increased to eight. They had fanned out and were coming across the open ground at a steady, purposeful lope. They looked tough and threatening and sure of themselves.

"There's just a chance," I said. "Where the cliff turned, I think I saw a break in the face. It may go right up."

We ran back. I had been right. There was a narrow cleft or chimney or couloir or what-have-you running into and across the rock face. It was wide enough to admit our bodies. Its surface was broken and irregular. There were almost certain to be hand and footholds.

"Can you climb?" I asked her.

"I can try."

"Up you go then. Quick."

She squeezed inside. Reaching up, she felt for a grip and found one. She began to climb. It seemed to be fairly easy going, at first anyway. After she had gone about ten feet I followed her. Before I went I turned to look back. The legionnaires were near, too damn near. The curve of the rock might conceal us. I hoped so.

Halfway up the rock face the couloir bent in a corner. I thought this might stop her. She paused for a moment, searching for a way around. I waited panting, hanging there, looking downward. Footsteps went by below me and I heard a gruff order given. Then she found what she was looking for and went on.

Once around the corner the shaft widened and we made better progress. It was not much more than a scramble, except for the final few feet. The fissure suddenly narrowed and went straight up like the chimney of a house. Again she paused. Below her I leaned out and looked up. She would have to get a grip on the top and pull or push herself the rest of the way. That is what she tried to do. And as she thrust herself upward her foothold gave way.

A sizeable piece of rock came crashing down and missed my right ear by an inch. It banged on its way from wall to wall collecting other pieces as it went and making a noise like a minor avalanche. "That's torn it," I thought.

I braced myself to catch her body as she fell and somehow stop us both from crashing to the bottom. But she didn't fall. She slammed against the rock face and I heard her cry out. Then her fingers found something to catch and held. I pushed my way up. Getting my shoulders under her feet I held her there. We were safe for the moment. Safe from falling, but not from anything else. We were at a stop, caught, stuck in the damned thing.

"Can you go on if I give you a lift?" I said.

"No," she was panting from the strain of holding herself there. "I can't."

"Why not?"

"I can't reach it, Richard. It's too far. I'm not strong enough."

There were noises at the bottom of the cliff. That avalanche had given us away, as I had known it would. They knew where we were now. Unless we made the top we were in a trap.

"Look, you've got to."

"No, I can't, I tell you. I can't."

More noises below told me that someone had started to climb after us.

I glanced up. There was a blue and cloudless sun-burnished sky above the mouth of the couloir. But it wasn't that I was looking at. I wanted to see if by any chance there was room to get past her. I thought there just was.

"Wait a bit," I said, as calmly as I could. Then I took her feet one by one from my shoulders and pushed them home on holds beside me. "Can you stay like that?"

"Yes, for a minute, I think. What are you going to do? Hurry, Richard."

I turned to the rock face on my own side and began to climb. Our bodies brushed and then jammed in the confined space. We were pinned together back to back. Sweat poured off me. If I slipped now I'd bring her with me, and we'd both go down into the arms of the waiting killers below.

I saw one of her hands slip and heard her cry out as I flattened myself, reached upward, and wrenched myself clear. Then I was lying face downward on the worn flat earth at the top of the cliff. I leaned down into the couloir. "Catch my hands," I said.

She came up when I pulled. She weighed nothing at all, which was just as well. I swung her up and clear, and she lay panting and gasping beside me.

"You didn't leave me," she said.

"We never do that on the playing fields of Eton," I said. "Besides, I want you for myself too damn much."

I looked over my shoulder. More patches of scrub grew some yards away. "Go and lie down in there," I told her.

"What are you going to do now, Général?"

"I'm about to see if this pop gun of yours is any good."

Sounds of heavy boots on stones, the clanging of iron on rock, grunts and vituperation were coming from the couloir.

I took the little gun from my pocket and put off the safety catch. Crawling nearer the edge, I stretched myself flat. My

175

heart was banging and my hand was still shaking from the climb. The point of the gun wandered around like a seismograph in a hurricane. That wasn't much good. I caught my right wrist in my left hand and held it steady, which made things a bit better.

A ridge of white showed above the edge of the rock. I held the tiny foresight on it as best I could and squinted down the little barrel. The line of white grew bigger and became the round flat top of a kepi. My heart had come down to nearer normal now and my hands were steadier. I squeezed the trigger. A tiny black hole appeared in the white. I put another shot into the edge of the couloir. A little puff of earth and stones shot up. The kepi disappeared. I turned and ran.

We were on a small plateau. We had, perhaps, two or three minutes start. I didn't deceive myself. The men who were after us were not undisciplined thugs or hoodlums to be disconcerted when they saw their quarry fighting back. They were trained soldiers and killers. Two .25 bullets at close range were not going to hold them up for long. They'd be out of that couloir and after us in battle order once they had their breath.

A dried-up watercourse suddenly appeared in front of us. I pulled her into it. "Keep down," I said.

The watercourse led us over the edge of the plateau and into a valley below. We made our way as best we could over the sharp, brittle rocks. There was cover here. Trees grew around us and over us. Soon we were in another small and sheltered valley. It was stifling hot and both of us were feeling tired. But my spirits began to rise a little. They couldn't possibly see us in this thickly wooded place. They would have to cast about again and guess which way we had gone. Moreover, a glance at the sun told me that the valley was leading us in the right direction. We were making progress, even if it was only in a small way.

The valley ended abruptly and with it the trees. A stretch of open country lay before us. We paused to take stock. There were no sights or sounds of pursuit. I looked back the way we had come and could see no one on the heights.

"We'll have to cross it," I said, "and we'll have to run. Can you?"

A thorn had ripped a red scratch across her cheek; her jeans were torn and slashed by the undergrowth; her shirt had come untucked and hung all awry; her hands were bleeding from the climb through the couloir. "I don't know," she said. "Can't we stay here?"

"No. We've got to get to Ajaccio and that's our direction. Apart from that, these people are trained hunters. We're only guessing we've lost them. They may be in the brush behind us. Are you ready?"

She ran her tongue over her lips. "Yes, Richard. All right."

We walked out into the full glare of the blinding sun. I estimated that it was about a quarter of a mile to the far ridge. "Run," I said.

It may have looked like English down country, but it wasn't. Ankle-high thorns caught at our feet; coarse grass wrapped around our legs; rocks and holes and hillocks impeded our stride. The sun burned us and drained us of energy.

We hadn't covered a quarter of the distance before we were panting and gasping. My legs felt like paper, as if they could no longer carry weight. She slowed to a walk and stopped.

"I don't know that I can make it," she panted, looking to the further crest. We certainly didn't seem to have gotten much nearer.

"Do you want me to carry you?" I said.

"No, damn you. Go on yourself."

"Do you know what they'll do when they catch up with you? They'll take time out to rape you. Perhaps that's what you want."

She pushed back her hair, damp and soaking with sweat. "Damn you, Graham," she said. "And damn you again."

She fell and I picked her up. I cursed her slowly and methodically with all the words I could dredge from memory. She went on. I remembered from my schooldays that you should push not pull a runner. I put my hand in the small of her back and pushed her.

177

We were about twenty yards from the crest when I heard the helicopter again. She looked back and gave a little cry. She did fall then, properly. I picked her up and carried her over the crest.

We both rolled together into the scant shade of a clump of thorn.

The helicopter passed low overhead. Of course, I thought. Once they'd lost the scent they would summon it to help them. At least that was one hazard a fox didn't have to face. The copter turned away, back toward the plateau.

My head was singing. I was sick from the sun and weak from exhaustion. She lay alongside me, her head on her hands. I turned to take stock of the situation. I thought it wouldn't be a bad idea if I made myself think like a fox. It was then that I saw the river.

Down to our left it flowed, not a hundred yards away, guarded by reeds and bamboos. The helicopter had gone by on its turn. I knew damn well what a fox would do. I jerked her to her feet.

"Quick," I said. "We have a chance of throwing them off."

She swayed as she got up. The sun was like another, additional enemy, remorseless, inescapable, burning us up. Somehow I hustled and dragged her across the open space to the shelter of the reeds and bamboos.

"We've got to get to the other side of this," I said.

It was a wide river. The banks were high and the soft-flowing water dark brown and greasy. The helicopter returned to direct the hunt. Here, near the river, sheltered by the high, thick bamboos, we were hidden from the eyes of its crew—or I thought we were.

She looked up at the copter and then down at the river. "I can't, Graham," she said. "I can't. I can't."

22

To the Death

She was on the verge of hysteria. So was I. "You're General Celle's daughter," I said. "Get into that stream." Then I hit her. I hit her as hard as I could with my open palm against the side of her face.

She staggered and recovered. Her eyes opened wide. A sort of shudder ran through her. She began to walk toward the bank. As we scrambled down I moved to help her.

"Don't touch me, damn you," she said.

Then we were in the water. The current was surprisingly strong. But it was cool and reviving. We let it carry us down. In a moment or so we were bumping against the farther side.

I felt for a hold, missed one and caught another. She was going away from me, but then she, too, caught a growing root and pulled herself up. In a minute we were both in the shelter of the far-side bamboos. Parting them, I looked back the way we had come.

A line of white kepis was approaching the bank we had just left.

They were fitter, stronger, tougher than we were. A wave of desperation caught me. The sun blazed down through the bamboos. I thought for an instant I was going to be sick, as nausea took me and I stood dripping half-cold from the river, half-roasted by the sun, dizzy, exhausted, frightened. Even if we did get to Ajaccio, I asked myself, what good could we do? Who was going to believe our story? If Gregorov's bogus legionnaires were prepared to carry their bluff through we might even find ourselves handed back to them. A mad impulse—one which I think comes at some time to most hunted things—to stand and shoot it out with the little gun came to me.

I put it aside. That way lay suicide, plain and simple, that was just what they wanted. I looked at her. She was shivering. She, too, was frightened. Exhaustion had given her that paper-thin, ethereal look which it does to fine-boned faces. Her eyes were enormous. She just wasn't made for this sort of thing. Her physical resources were running out. She seemed lost and defenseless. Although I knew she was neither, something about her caught at my throat. Those legionnaires were not going to have her while I was still on my feet.

The white kepis were in the bamboos now and moving through them. If both they and the helicopter failed to spot us, they would have to spend some time puzzling out our trail. What would a fox do? He'd run the river in the direction of his point. If I got out of this I swore I'd never go fox-hunting again.

"We'd better move on," I said.

I took her arm and this time she did not resist me. We began to make our way downstream as best we could through the reeds and bamboos.

Twice the helicopter clattered overhead. It seemed to have lost us and to be searching. At a bend in the river I looked back. Two of the white kepis were swimming across, their automatic weapons held above their heads. That meant they must have split up. They had lost us all right. Two were better odds than eight. We pushed on.

After about half an hour we had to leave the river when it turned almost completely on itself to begin its long fall down to the sea. We struggled on over several open ridges. At one point we passed a line of notices with the legend CHASSE GARDEE in yellow letters on a black background. I didn't think Gregorov's toughs would pay much attention to them. At intervals we could hear and sometimes see the helicopter behind us. It was clearly at a loss and was either covering ground we had already traversed or searching the way we hadn't gone.

But the heat hadn't abated. The sun was very high and the going dreadfully rough. Our clothes had long since dried on us and, now stiff and soiled, were rubbing at our roughened skins. She was moving more and more slowly with every step she took, and I wasn't doing much better. I hated the sun with a vicious, personal hatred. All I could do was to keep myself going over the rocks and through the harsh, coarse grass. And I doubted if I'd be able to do this for much longer. Then she tripped and fell once more. I bent over her and pulled her to her feet.

It was no good. We had to have rest and shade. We had been on the run now for over six hours. That would get to the heart of any fox. What would he do in circumstances such as these? He'd find somewhere to lie up and rest and regain his strength. An old water tank, the top of a wall, the branch of a tree— that's what he'd look for. None of those were any good to us, but we'd gained time and ground, which was what a fox had when he searched for these refuges. We must look for one too.

And then I saw the mine chimney. It pushed up just over a ridge to our right. Beside it was the roofless top of a tall building.

"What's that?" I said to her, pointing.

"It's probably an old silver mine. The Germans destroyed them all when they left. They've never been reopened."

The clatter of the helicopter sounded again; it seemed to be coming nearer. I caught her shoulder. "Run," I said, "run as you've never run before."

We staggered rather than ran over the summit of the little hill. Down below us were the empty, windowless mine buildings. An overgrown light railway, its tracks torn up and awry, curled toward a dark opening in the hillside. I half-pulled, half-carried her toward it.

As we reached its welcoming darkness the blades of the helicopter went swishing overhead. We stood for a moment or two getting our breaths and then walked further into the depths of the mineshaft. Soon there was water around our ankles and the sleepers of the railway became rotten under our feet. Rats scampered away from us with horrible scratching sounds.

"You do pick the nicest places, Graham," she said.

"Yes, well, times are tough all over, as Roddy would say."

The light grew less and then, as the shaft turned, we were in total darkness. A fallen bank of timber barred our way. I stepped over this and came upon a jumble of props where the roof had come in. That seemed far enough. We could find a place to rest on the timber.

"And now?" she said.

"Wait. Rest if we can. Get some steam into us. Then, when it's cooler, try again."

"I seem to have gotten you into something, don't I, Graham?"

"We'll get out of it."

"I wonder. Did they see us?"

"I don't think so. If they did, the first man around that corner there is going to find out that little gun of yours can kill at close range. Try to rest."

But she couldn't rest. Instead she talked. It was as if strain and exhaustion had set off some spring of speech inside her. She talked of loneliness and fear, of being brought up alone by elderly parents in an atmosphere of resentment, disillusion, and bitterness, of her love for her father and her own increasing toughness and hardness as she saw all he had lived by falling to ashes around him. She had gone on loving him and serving him, hating herself for the things she was doing and hating more the people she was doing them for. But she had done them and soon, to her horror, had found herself taking pleasure in doing them successfully. Yet despite the horror, which gradually grew less as she grew older and harder, that feeling of successful accomplishment was the only thing that kept her spirit alive at all. I knew just how she felt.

"Two of a kind, Graham," she whispered to me. Her fingers felt inside my shirt and traced again the outline of my scars. For

182

an instant in that dark and reeking passage our worn, tired bodies clung together as we tried to comfort and take strength from each other. Then she drew away. "You have to pay," she said. "You always have to pay. At least we have. Where there is honor there is payment for dishonor. My father knew that. He proved it."

"Look," I said, "wake up. We're not at Roncesvalles now." I took her by the shoulders and shook her. "We're going to beat this thing, you and I, and get through. And I'm no bloomin' Bayard, remember that."

She laughed then. "Your history is a little mixed, Graham," she said. "But that you're not. You don't understand honor. No Englishman does. You're a shopkeeper like the rest of your nation."

"If you're not very careful I'll hit you again."

It was time to go. Together we made our way to the mouth of the shaft. The fierce heat had gone. That was the first thing we noticed. A cool, sweet evening breeze came off the maquis.

There was no one around. No white kepi stood sentinel over the buildings. We came out slowly, blinking, into the light. The mine lay in a hollow in the hills. A worn track, largely grass-grown, which must once have been a road, led away from it around a spur of rock.

I looked at the sun. "That track has to lead to a road," I said. "Ajaccio is in that direction, too." I pointed to the southwest. "There's no sign of them at the moment. I think we should follow the track. It must lead somewhere. If we reach a road maybe we could grab a lift. Perhaps they've given up."

"Gregorov never gives up," she said.

We walked along, waiting every instant for the sight of those white kepis springing up from the maquis. The track twisted and turned among the hillocks and ridges. Then, quite suddenly, it ended.

We were on a tiny, narrow road that sloped steeply downward. The surface had been freshly tarred so it must, I thought, lead somewhere. If so, we might find help and shelter. We began to walk along it. After we had covered about a mile we came around two hairpin turns and then the road broadened and became level for a distance of fifty yards or so. A wall ran along the far side and beyond the wall was a trim square château. The gate to the château was locked and barred and the windows were shuttered. There were well-kept terraces of vines in front of it and a little further on the entrance to the vineyard. At this entrance was an open Fiat with running boards, high-pressure tires, and outside headlights. It was thirty-five years old if it was a day. But whoever owned it had cared for it well. It looked as if it had just come from the showroom.

"We've got transportation at any rate," I said, opening the door and getting inside. She sat beside me.

I switched on the ignition and the engine started immediately. No one shouted at us. I let in the clutch. We were off on what I hoped was the last lap of our journey.

The wind came curling around the straight windshield and caressed and cooled us. The road was falling all the way. The engine gave off a healthy song. We topped a rise and down below us was the fertile valley before Ajaccio. The main road to the city ran across the further side. At the bottom of the valley another road joined ours. Both were free of traffic.

Our road straightened into a long slope. I pressed the accelerator. The old car gained speed like a horse lengthening his stride. This was open motoring at its best.

"You should have a bonnet and a dust coat," I said. "Next stop Ajaccio."

At that moment the cursed helicopter came at us again. What with the noise made by the engine and the wind I hadn't heard it until it was slap on top of 'us.

"We can beat it yet," I said, putting on more speed and making for the high road.

And then I saw the big brown camion racing along the valley to cut us off.

I slammed on the brakes. The car took a bit of time to stop. Brakes in those more leisurely days of motoring went on the principle of slow retrogression. There wasn't so much traffic around then, which was just as well.

"Hold it," I said, when we were down to about fifteen miles an hour, and the camion was almost at the cross. "I'll have to ditch her."

I slid the car sideways into the bank. That stopped her good and proper. The car tore away the grass and growth, hit a rock, and canted sideways into the road, blocking it.

Then we were on the run again. And this time we had no start at all.

A burst of submachine gun fire ripped after us as we dived into the scrub. They must be pretty desperate, I thought, to risk it here, so near to civilization.

There were paths through this particular clump of trees and undergrowth. Moreover, the ground on either side was broken up into fields and hedgerows. We still had a chance if we could get into them and make the road. But the sounds of pursuit were very close. From scent to view, I thought stupidly, as I ran.

We met a small stream, forded it, and pelted along a path. We were now nearing the final rise to the road. There was only a field between us and it. We had to cross it—just one field.

A legionnaire in camouflage uniform suddenly appeared slap in front of us, blocking the path. He came out of the maquis and stood there huge and threatening. He was about five feet away. He swung his carbine up.

I had the little gun in my hand. I shot him twice in the stomach. He doubled up, his lips stretched in a livid grin. It was the chap with the cicatrice who had hit me on the road.

We ran on. We were in the field now. The final rise was only a few yards away.

Then, suddenly, things began to happen all together.

First, a ring of white kepis appeared in a half-circle behind us in the field. Leading them was an officer with a 9mm. Mauser in his hand. It was Gregorov. He shouted to us to stop.

I turned and fired the little gun. My hand was waving around like a branch in the wind; the gun wasn't made for this sort of work. I fired too soon anyway. I was rattled. I missed. Gregorov laughed and raised the big Mauser. He stood there, straddle-legged, in the pistol-shooting position, a gloating look on his face.

Beside me I heard her cry out. I turned. The road was lined with military vehicles. Two men were standing at its edge. One of them had a sporting rifle at his shoulder.

The two shots rang out almost simultaneously. In front of me Gregorov's face erupted in a mass of blood. At the same instant she staggered and cried again. She crumpled up slowly, quietly, a look almost of surprise on her face. I ran to her as she fell and bent over her on the ground. Her hand, in a vain effort, was trying to cover the hole in her side where the big Mauser bullet from Gregorov's gun had gone home. She was ashen white. Her eyes opened and then her lips.

"It hurts; God, it hurts," she said. She tried to smile. "I never really thought we'd make it, Bayard," she said.

"But we did," I said. "Take it easy."

I picked her up and carried her to the road.

Simon Herald was lowering the Mannlicher to the ground when I came up. Beside him an officer in a Major's kepi was barking orders. Khaki-clad men were spilling into the fields.

"I got the message, but I had a hell of a job convincing these men," Simon said. "The helicopter led us to you in the end. I knew I'd get into this game somehow."

"You were a little late, chum," I said. I carried her on down the line of cars. When they saw what had happened they made way for us. Someone gave an urgent order. An empty camion started up, spun on its tracks, and pointed back the way it had come. Hands helped us in. An N.C.O. came running with a sulpha pack. I laid her down as gently as I could. The camion began to go very fast toward Ajaccio. She was still breathing.

She died that night. I stayed with her all the time and she fought her going every inch of the way. Only once, for a brief instant, did she regain consciousness and that was very near the end. Her eyes opened and she looked at me. She suddenly seemed just as I had known her before, full of life, vitality, and challenge.

"Times are tough all over, Graham," she said very clearly and mockingly. Then the moment of clarity passed as quickly as it had come. Her eyes closed and the labored breathing became worse. Shortly after that it ceased.

I went blindly out into the darkened corridor. I would never know whether he had aimed at and shot her or whether she had shielded me, and the recollection of that scene below the road would be with me all my life.

They made me go to a room and gave me a slug of something to make me sleep. It didn't; I never expected it would. I don't think they did either. That must have been why they had a young officer share my room. They said it was for company, and I suppose in a way it was.

Next morning there were formalities to be gone through about charging McKee—though they didn't seem to be all that keen about this—and making a long statement about what I had done and knew and guessed. I did it all like a man in a dream, or rather a nightmare.

They had rounded up Gregorov's renegades with the efficiency and ruthlessness they always display when the chips are down. They seemed unwilling to tell me anything, I suppose because they thought I knew too much already.

Then they flew me back to London. They seemed to think it would be as well if I got away as soon as possible. It was, they implied, and I agreed with them, a domestic matter and one for them to settle themselves. I had become involved in it purely at the request of this one or that, and quite unofficially. In a scrupulously polite way they made quite certain that I did not miss my plane. Nor did they intend that I should fail to make the connection at Nice. One of them traveled with me in the Caravelle and bought me lunch at Nice airport. I thought of telling him that if he had to lug all that artillery around with him an under-the-shoulder holster and a lightweight suit were not the best combination for concealment. I didn't. Instead I bought *The Times* at the newsstand and read it ostentatiously throughout luncheon. I also drank champagne at his expense. The waiter said it was *trop cher,* but I thought it the best drink for a man in a nightmare. It tasted like off-key soda water mixed with sawdust. That was part of the nightmare, I supposed.

It was while I was drinking it—or trying to—that I heard someone stop at our table.

"Champagne, indeed," said a voice I knew. "I'm rather partial to a glass in the morning myself, just for my stomach's sake. Mind if I join you?"

I looked up. It was Roddy. He pulled out a chair and sat down.

"Have a go," I said. "It's all on M. le Général it seems."

"I see. Damn generous of him, I'm sure. If that's the case, what about ordering up another? You'd better get something out of this, Richard. I don't somehow see him giving you that red pin or whatever that you stick in your buttonhole."

My escort was shoving forward his left shoulder with the artillery underneath it and fingering his chin and looking restive.

"Relax," I said to him. "This is a friend of mine. He has no political ideas. In fact he doesn't know what politics are. *Il aime beaucoup les chevaux de course.*"

Roddy grinned. "What does that mean?" he said. "I'm sure it's rude."

"Where did you spring from anyway? You do have a way of bobbing up, don't you?"

"I came over earlier and waited for you. I had an idea you'd be coming through from Sue. It seemed to me it might be a bit rough for you alone after everything. I didn't realize you'd have company."

"Not for long, I think. He's just seeing me off the premises. And, thanks, chum."

"That's all right, Richard. How do you feel? A bit as if you'd taken a header?"

"You can say that again."

A jet took off with a strident scream from what seemed like a few feet away.

"Hellish noisy hereabouts," Roddy said. "And you can't get *Sporting Life* at the newsstand. I'm not sure I like abroad all that much."

We were called just then. I couldn't deny that I was grateful to him. I hadn't relished the idea of the journey home with only my thoughts for company.

In the airplane Roddy ordered more champagne. We laced it with brandy and I began to think I could taste things again. I paid. He had had, it seemed, to borrow the money for his ticket home from Simon.

"And the damn fellow didn't seem all that sorry to lend it, either," he said. "Almost as if he was glad enough to see me go, if you can believe it."

"I believe it all right. He probably thought it was cheap at the price. What happened to all the folding stuff you won in Nice?"

"That? I lost all that in the little casino in Ajaccio one night. Playing boule, too, of all things. I say, Richard, I believe I could use another brandy, could you?"

At London Airport an elderly gentleman called Sir William Bellamy, whom I had met before and who combined some interesting duties with a Fellowship of All Souls, was waiting for me in the lounge. He looked at Roddy. "And who may this be?" he asked.

"A certain R. Marston, Gentleman Rider," I said.

"Indeed." He studied Roddy more closely. "I didn't think such people existed any more," he said.

"They don't," Roddy told him. "Richard is a bit old-fashioned. Nowadays none of us are gentlemen and precious few of us are riders."

"Fancy." He turned to me. "Well, now," he said, "if your friend will excuse us, I'm afraid I must have a few words with you alone, my dear boy."

As I turned to go, Roddy touched me on the arm. "Look, Richard," he said awkwardly, "it can't be much fun for you just now. Tommy Jarrett and I have half-shares in a second-stringer we're trying to get ready for Lewes or somewhere. It's at his place. Come down and help us, Richard. It'll do you good."

"Thanks. I'll do that. Ring the flat, will you?"

Sir Richard led me quickly through customs and down to where a pre-war Rolls was waiting. "Is he any good?" he asked me reflectively as we settled ourselves on the cushions.

"Who, Roddy?"

"Yes."

"As a rider?"

"You didn't imagine, I suppose, that I was asking as a solicitor or a dentist or an auctioneer, did you? Yes, as a rider."

"The living best, that's all."

"I see." The expression crossed his features which meant that he was pigeonholing a piece of information, perhaps for future use. Then he turned to me. He knew all about what had happened.

It transpired he wanted to offer me permanent employment. I accepted. Manahan had called me an anachronism and he had been right. I had been playing the half-hearted, the uncommitted for too long. It was time I came to terms with today. I was finished with being an amateur—for always.

Welcome, John   Copy 1 ✓
Wanted for killing.

1-68